The Cloak Of Feathers

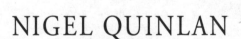

NIGEL QUINLAN

Orion
Children's Books

ORION CHILDREN'S BOOKS

First published in Great Britain in 2018
by Hodder and Stoughton

3 5 7 9 10 8 6 4 2

Text © Nigel Quinlan, 2018

The moral rights of the author have been asserted.

A CIP catalogue record for this book
is available from the British Library.

ISBN 978 1 4440 1418 1

Typeset by Input Data Services Ltd, Somerset

Printed and bound in Great Britain
by Clays Ltd, St Ives plc

The paper and board used in this book are from well-managed forests
and other responsible sources.

MIX
Paper from
responsible sources
FSC® C104740

Orion Children's Books
An imprint of
Hachette Children's Group
Part of Hodder and Stoughton
Carmelite House
50 Victoria Embankment
London EC4Y 0DZ

An Hachette UK Company
www.hachette.co.uk

www.hachettechildrens.co.uk

To the organisers of festivals of all types and themes, little and large, who work so hard to bring a little fun to our lives. They're the real Good Folk who make Festivals Great.

Part One:
Friday

1.

FETCHING THE COW

I TOLD THEM I'd go and fetch the stupid cow.

We were sitting round the table in the living room of the Bellamore house, behind their shop, completely surrounded by piles and piles of Sheila Bellamore's Festival Bread, which she and Bob had been baking all week. The Bellamore Festival Bread was black as soot, tasted like a fireplace and had a crust hard enough to shatter teeth. Through a nearby door I could see that the floor of their kitchen was hidden under an untidy clutter of open sacks and large tubs. The sacks were full of dark, crumbly stuff, some of which smelled like peat, some like coal dust and some like nothing at all on this earth. The tubs were full of molasses and, maybe, engine oil. Those were her ingredients.

'Well done, Brian,' said Bob, Sheila's husband. Bob was always hugely encouraging when other people offered to do things.

'Why don't you take Derek and Helen with you?' said Mum, who was always full of helpful suggestions that made everyone's lives so simple and easy. 'You can be the

Junior Action (Cow Fetching) Sub Group. Here, I'll make stickers.'

'Oh yes, I'd love to!' That was Helen Kelly, Bob and Sheila's niece. Prim and alert, she watched everyone and everything with eager eyes. She was wearing jodhpurs, boots and a riding jacket; Helen was always coming from, or on her way to, something to do with horses. I sometimes had the feeling she was taking valuable time out of her important horse-related activities to check that the bumbling peasants weren't making a complete mess out of everything. Sticking her chin into the air and a sticker on her lapel she looked at Derek and me as if we were a pair of lazy ponies about to be taken for a trot.

'I'll make sure it's done properly and that nothing goes wrong this time!' she promised.

I opened my mouth to protest that *actually* nothing had gone wrong the other times (mostly), but I was interrupted by a loud burp.

'I'd rather saw my own leg off and have it for dinner,' said Derek Bellamore. ''Scuse me.'

He was slouched across a chair like a lean streak of meanness, wearing a green tracksuit a size too big for him. His hands were in his pockets, his shoulders were hunched, and he was chanting a rap song under his breath as if it were an incantation. Derek had been forced onto the Festival committee by Sheila and Bob as part of his 'community service' for stealing bicycles. He'd stolen my beloved Backahatchi 3000 and either rode it like a demon through hell or driven a steamroller over it, because it was a ruined mess when I got it back.

'Great! You three get the cow and we'll meet you down at the Green in half an hour,' said Dad. 'Watch out for Mulkytine!'

Ah, Dad. He has a talent for saying the wrong thing at the wrong time. Sheila gasped and pursed her lips with intense disapproval. Bob went pale and shook his head from side to side for about ten seconds before he found his voice.

'Oh no, Gerald,' he said, almost whispering. 'Don't go saying *his* name on the eve of the Festival! If *he* hears you, he'll come and find you! Don't ever talk about him!'

'Sorry,' said Dad, hunching up a bit, the way you do when a joke falls really flat. 'Forget I said anything.'

I look a bit like a small version of my dad, except I keep my hair cut short and I wear loose baggy clothes: combat trousers, t-shirts a few sizes too big for me, and tough boots laced up tight. I'm told I frown a lot and should smile more often. *You* try smiling more often when people keep wrinkling their noses at you as if you haven't washed in weeks, even though you shower every day. You try living where we live.

'We'll say no more about it,' said Sheila. 'Have some bread before you go?'

I wasn't sure if she was talking about her Festival Bread or ordinary regular bread. We all said no, just to be safe.

All together, Mum, Dad, Sheila and Bob were the sensible grown-up Knockmealldown Festival Committee, while us silly wee twelve-year-olds were the Junior Action (Cow Fetching) Sub Group.

Helen's parents had more sense than to get involved.

They usually booked themselves a foreign holiday at Festival time. This year Helen had resolved to stay with her aunt, uncle and cousin to help out. It was her first festival. She was horribly excited about it. I tried to warn her, but she wouldn't listen. Now I was stuck with her and Derek for the first big job. Fetching the cow.

The Knockmealldown Summer Festival was starting the next day, and we couldn't start the festival without the cow. All through the weekend the cow would wander up and down the village and people would bet on where she'd make a mess. This was the most popular activity of the Festival. In fact, it was the only activity of the Festival that was even remotely popular. So we had to have the cow.

Normally I didn't mind. Fetching the cow was probably the least horrible of all the Festival jobs, even if I did have to go through Ghost Pig Estate to do it. What I minded was having Derek and Helen come with me.

The first obstacle on our journey was geting the heck out of the Bellamore house. Sheila and Bob's Festival Bread was heaped against the walls to elbow height, leaving only a narrow passage between, forcing us to walk sideways as we left. There were rolls of it piled in every corner, scattered around the floor like cannonballs in a gunpowder magazine. I could see them stacked along the hallway and going up the stairs, and more in the sitting room and more on the table and counters in the kitchen. There were hundreds of rolls of black bread, smelling of warm treacle and turf and coal-dust. I heard the timer on the oven go *ping* as another batch was finished.

6

Sheila persisted in making huge quantities of this stuff every year to be sold at the Festival Market. It was the only thing ever sold at the Festival Market. Except none of it was ever actually sold. There was a dark and brooding mountain of it growing in the local landfill. Mum and Dad tried to gently convince her that it was all just a tiny bit wasteful, but Sheila ignored them.

'There's always been bread at the Festival,' she'd say. 'If there's none of my bread at the market on Sunday morning certain folk won't be happy and there'll be trouble, mark my words.' Bob agreed with his wife, so that was it. There would be bread.

2.
WHAT WE TALK ABOUT WHEN WE TALK ABOUT THE GOOD FOLK

'WHAT IN THE name of all that's manky and rotten do we want with this amount of bread anyway?' demanded Derek, jabbing a pile of rolls with his elbow, then gasping with pain. 'Every year it's the same. The house smells like a garage for weeks. If one fell on you it'd break your leg. Can't even eat the stuff.'

'It's traditional!' said Helen. 'Isn't this the bread for the Fairy Breakfast?'

'HOLY MACKEREL!' roared Derek, stopping us abruptly in our tracks. It was a bit loud, even for him. 'Don't you know anything or is all that hair growing straight out of your brain? You don't ever call 'em that!'

'Call who what?' said Helen. 'The fairies? Oops!' She clapped her hands over her mouth.

'Oh, jaypers, you giddy twit!' Derek put his hands on his head and danced a little jig of frustration. 'Not here! You can't be doing that here! They'll steal our teeth or swap our hands with our feet! Call them the Little People! The Good Folk! The Gentry! The Other Crowd! Call them Rover and

8

Fido, for all I care! Just don't call them by the *f* word!'

'I'm so sorry!' Helen. 'I completely forgot! I've just never understood why they should be bothered by people calling them by their real name.'

'Ask them tomorrow, if they show up. Just wait till I've caught a plane to America before you do. They don't like it and that's that!'

'Derek's right, Helen,' Bob called from the living room. 'For once!'

'Yes, please don't use that word,' said Sheila. 'Especially not tomorrow . . .'

Inside I knew Mum and Dad were trying very hard not to roll their eyes at the Magic Name Police.

'Oh, yes, tomorrow!' said Helen, and she clapped her hands with the doomed delight of someone who had never attended a Knockmealldown Summer Festival before. 'Do you really think they'll come to the Festival?'

I put my hands over my face for a moment. Knockmealldown was a thick, lumpy soup of legends and stories. Just having a conversation around here was like walking through a maze with a mythical creature hidden round every corner. To hear some folk go on about it, you couldn't swing a cat in Knockmealldown without hitting a magical being, making them very angry and getting cursed or eaten or turned into a cabbage. There was Mulkytine, the Boar of Lisashee, who escaped from the Otherworld and rampaged over seven counties a thousand years ago. Supposedly it was this same mad, giant, magical boar that had come back ten years ago to smash the local pig factory to smithereens, free all the pigs and led them on a piggy riot all over the village. But it was the legend of the great Festival that had everyone excited at the moment. Every hundred years the fair– the Gentle Folk emerged from the Otherworld to take part in the Knockmealldown Summer Festival, a weekend full of magic and craic! They reckoned it had been a hundred years since the last one, so the Good Folk were even now putting on their glad rags and heading for Knockmealldown. So, yes, the Good Folk were going to be here. Tomorrow.

The Knockmealldown Summer Festival. The worst festival in the country, if not the world, if not the universe. The only festival on the National Tourist Board's online list of summer festivals marked with a big red AVOID.

Mum and Dad had been helping run the Knockmealldown Festival since we'd moved here three years before. It's the sort of thing they do: getting involved with the local community, helping out, doing their bit, giving something back. Which meant I had to do the same, whether I wanted to or not. After my first Festival, I would sooner have volunteered to go searching for land mines on a pogo stick than do it again. There had been no magic, no wonder and definitely no fai— Other Folk. The weather was awful, the food was inedible, the music was a disaster and the games and activities were catastrophes. The only thing that ever went right was the cow making the mess.

'We need a stick,' Derek suddenly decided as we went out of the Bellamore's house and through their small shop. He stopped and glared around as if searching for the idiot who'd forgotten the stick, settling on me. I sighed. So it begins.

'What,' I asked, 'do we need a stick for?'

'And a rope,' Helen said.

'No! What? No!' I said. 'What do we need a rope for?'

Helen and Derek, who agreed on approximately absolutely nothing whatsoever, looked at each other with perfect understanding.

'We're going to fetch a cow, Brian,' said Helen. Helen enjoyed explaining obvious things to people who couldn't seem to understand them. She did it slowly, patiently and kindly, and it made my eyes boil in their sockets.

'A cow, Brian, a cow!' barked Derek. Derek, on the other hand, constantly flew into rages when other people turned out to be stupid, and other people turned out to be stupid ALL THE TIME.

'You know, big four-legged thing with a tail, always eatin' the grass? That's a cow, Brian! How are you goin' to fetch the flippin' thing if you don't know what it looks like?'

'I know what a cow looks like,' I said. I had fetched the cow last year AND the year before all by myself, with no help or support from a thick-headed hooligan or a horsey princess who thought they knew better than everyone else.

'He knows what a cow looks like,' Helen explained patiently to Derek. 'He just doesn't know how to handle one, and that in order to fetch one, he needs a rope which can be used to fashion a crude bridle with which to lead the cow. It's lucky I'm here. My experience with horses will be invaluable. We won't be needing a stick, Derek. I don't approve of animal cruelty.'

'Get away with your rope and your crude bridle,' said

Derek. 'A good whack on the backside with a skelp o' wood'll show her who's boss in short order. And what are you talkin' about, animal cruelty? Last I checked you were huntin' foxes for sport!'

'First of all, cattle respond better to gentle persuasion than to violence and brutality. Second of all, we only ever do drag hunting, so no foxes are ever harmed on any of my hunts, though the smelly bag that gets dragged does suffer some wear and tear. Third of all—'

'Third of all we don't need a rope, fourth of all we don't need a stick and fifth of all, come on if you're coming!' I said, my patience snapping like a Jolly Roger in a stiff breeze. I turned on my heel and marched through the door of Bob and Sheila's shop, hoping they wouldn't follow, knowing they would. Knowing that the whole way there and back they'd only stop arguing with each other to gang up on me.

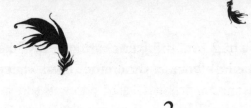

3.

KNOCKMEALLDOWN

WE WALKED DOWN Main Street as if we had a purpose, which is something people walking down Main Street rarely had. First, though, we took off the stickers saying Junior Action (Cow Fetching) Sub Group and threw them in a bin. Well, Derek scrunched his up and threw it on the ground and then Helen made him pick it up and throw it in the bin.

Knockmealldown doesn't look so bad from outside Bellamore's Stores, near the top of the hill. The road winds and turns and bends like a stream in a meadow, and the houses line the road, old and crooked, some leaning out, some leaning back, with overhanging roofs and painted window-frames. The wooden doors have metal latches and all the stone walls are painted or white-washed. Smoke that smells of wood and turf trickles from the chimneys, and the window boxes are overflowing with flowers and vegetables.

When I first saw it, three years ago, I thought it was magical. Driving down that winding, crooked, fairy-tale street, a hazy mist hiding the Estate and the mud of the

Pond, the top of Long Lisa's Tower floating eerily like a glimpse into a magical faraway Otherland, I was actually thrilled.

I knew the stories: of the Great Festivals, the White Cow and the Black Boar, Mulkytine. Even the Curse that was supposed to have been put on the village by the Folk after the pig factory was built on their land twenty years ago, and the story of the rampaging pigs that destroyed the factory ten years later were thrilling to me. If nothing else, the place sounded *interesting*.

Sometimes, when the sun comes out and raindrops glitter on the eaves and steam rises like mist from the road and there's a hush, as if every breath is held, waiting for the moment to pass into something strange and wonderful, I remember that feeling, and wonder how I could ever have been so deluded.

Up close and three years after I first saw them, the houses on Main Street were all shabby and slightly crooked. They looked as tired and depressed as I usually felt, and they leaned on each other for support like wounded soldiers after a particularly pointless battle. Their windows were like drooping, dusty eyes, the sort of eyes you see in horrible paintings of sad clowns.

There'd been no work around here since the pigs wrecked the factory before stampeding around the village causing thousands of euros' worth of damage, then disappearing into the Mud Pond. Things had gone downhill from there. Most of the young people leave as soon as they're old enough to hitch a lift to the nearest bus stop. The people who stay have nothing to do but sit around all day feeling haunted and confused.

There are two pubs in Knockmealldown, Mulligan's and Tracey's, and they're next door to each other. They've been feuding ferociously since an argument over the answer to a question in a Sunday-night quiz in 1987. As we walked past, Tom Tracey and Tricia Mulligan were standing in their doorways ignoring each other. They were older than us and they liked to act like they owned the whole place, which, when you thought about it, wasn't that much to be proud of.

'Oh look, it's the Festival Committee,' said Tricia. 'God, not the bloody Festival again. Is it going to be another awful mess this year?'

'Oh God, what's going to go wrong this year?' moaned Tom. 'Are you going to sink another band in a bog? Lose another thirty runners on a Fun Run? It's in jail you should be!'

'I didn't think the Festival could get any worse,' said Tricia. 'But you'll manage somehow!'

'Oh, but this is going to be the *Great Festival*!' said Tom. 'Happens every hundred years! The Little People are comin'!'

I gritted my teeth and ignored them. The sinking band and the Fun Run disaster weren't my fault. Tom and Tricia laughed until they suddenly noticed they were laughing together; then they stopped abruptly and went back to ignoring each other and hating each other with the heat of a million suns.

Down from the pubs was Una's Hair and Beauty Salon. Una's uncle had been Mick Taffe, a legendary hurler in his time, one of the few famous people to come out of Knockmealldown. Una herself had trained as a hairdresser in Dublin, and she was actually really good. You weren't allowed to say so though, because that might draw the bad luck. When things got bad I sometimes went to Una's. Inside, it smelled of hot hair, shampoo and coffee. The chairs were comfortable, and I read magazines about beautiful people having lovely lives. The women there chatted about this and that, and everyone but Una pretended I wasn't there. I swept up the hair clippings and worked the till. She gave me tea and biscuits.

At the bottom of the hill was the Village Green and the lake of Lisashee. We called the lake the Mud Pond, because pollution from the pig factory had turned the water to pure, thick, brown filth. The Green had shrunk to a tiny strip of dying grass, and at one end there was a tiny, shabby workman's hut that housed the Knockmealldown Public Library.

A few dismal, shallow watercourses trickled along the surface of the mud; oily water the colour of dirty rainbows. They all pooled together round a small island in the middle of the Pond; the Isle of Lisashee. It was overgrown, with a thick impenetrable forest of hawthorn, and rising from the greenery was a tall, ivy-covered, melancholic, crow-infested castle. Long Lisa's Tower, crumbling away with a kind of fed-up dignity, lonely and neglected and forgotten.

There used to be a ferry across to the island, but nobody goes there any more because ferries and boats in general don't do well in mud, and also because the mud stank worse than a million stuck toilets all exploding in every direction at once. But the island was where the cow was kept, and that's where we had to go to fetch it.

The road that runs through Knockmealldown does not go all the way down to the Pond. It swerves left at the last minute and shoots straight as an arrow for about a mile, as if fleeing in terror. Long before my time, according to the locals, there used to be a pleasant little wood here, full of ancient trees with their roots sunk deep into the rich soil. A path meandered under their outstretched branches, taking wanderers, ramblers and strollers down to the Green and the Pond, back when it was still a lake.

Now, though, all the trees were gone, and two lonely, weather-stained concrete columns stood on either side of a nasty red gouge in the earth. What was once the loveliest place in Knockmealldown is now the worst, a place where no one ever goes if they don't have to – Ghost Pig Estate. It stood between us, the Pond and the cow.

'Hey, Brian,' Helen said, turning to smile brightly at me. 'Isn't this where you live?'

Derek snickered. I scowled.

'And aren't you the *only* people who live there?'

'Yeah,' I said. 'The only people.'

'Imagine, all those empty houses with nobody living in them,' she said. 'That must be spooky.'

'They're not empty,' I said,

'Yeah,' said Derek. 'They're full of rats.'

'That's not all they're full of,' I said. We stood at the gate, hesitating. A fog was thickening around us, fading the Estate to a grey haze until it was full of ghost houses.

If you had a choice between living in Ghost Pig Estate or living in Dracula's Castle, next door to Azkhaban, on the slopes of Mount Doom, I'd start stocking up on garlic if I were you.

The roads in the Estate were just stretches of hard, broken clay. So were the footpaths. And the gardens. And the floors of most of the houses. Everything here was hard, broken clay – except when it rained. Then it turned into a thick, sticky muck that never properly washed out of my shoes or my clothes or my skin or my hair. Una shaved my hair for me with a number two razor every month. I looked like a skinhead.

Derek sniffed the air with a mixture of awe and disgust. Even hardened Knockmealldowners find the atmosphere in the Estate a bit much.

The smell was the result of years' worth of pollution that had flowed out of the pig factory, choking the Pond to death, soaking into the earth, killing every living thing, stewing and rotting and stinking until there wasn't a molecule of clean air left. When the factory burned down the Estate had been built on the ruins, but the Smell had lingered like a bad memory that keeps you wide awake all night staring at the ceiling long after the event itself has been forgotten by everyone else. That's why no one ever bought a house or tried to live there until we came along, me and my madly optimistic parents who thought that for a house that cheap we could get used to a bit of pong. If anything, the smell was even worse in the Estate than in the Pond; a toxic gas that melted the hairs in your nose and stuck to the inside of your mouth and curled up in a thick pool in your chest. It actually weighed you down and made you feel like you were a bad person.

I had my hands in my pockets and my shoulders hunched. Helen was looking pale and prim, acting even more stiff and dainty than normal, as if she were trying to turn herself into a porcelain doll who didn't have to breathe. Nobody made a move to go any further.

Over the years, the Estate itself had been completely devoured by Norwegian Hëlweed, a weird invasive plant that sprounted not long after we moved in, quickly choking everything in yellow tendrils and scarlet flowers. Most of the houses were now just big yellow-green lumps, swamped by waves of weeds. My own home-sweet-home was the only building that wasn't filled with poisonous vegetation, but we kept an uneasy eye on the carpet of Hëlweed that was creeping hungrily across the road towards us. The tangle of evil plants had covered over a big pothole in the middle of the road, turning it into a deadly car trap as deep and wide as a paddling pool. It would have been incredibly dangerous if any cars ever made it that far into the Estate.

'Them pigs are running high today,' Derek said. 'Must be all excited for tomorrow.'

I didn't like to hear people talking about the pigs. It made me nervous.

'Oh, the pigs!' said Helen, as if she'd been trying to remember someone's name and just thought of it. 'This is where the pig factory was, isn't it? The one that the government built despite all the locals protesting because they said it would disturb the fai— '

Helen looked around, suddenly worried.

'Do you think the Other Folk'll still be angry?' she said. 'I mean, the pig factory polluted the lake and smelled awful, and after it closed down that developer came and half-built the Estate and all this horrible Hëlweed showed up.'

'Wasn't our fault!' declared Derek passionately. 'Outsiders came and ruined the whole place! That's why the Other Folk are so mad at us! Everyone knows they cursed Knockmealldown because of what them outsiders did! Bad luck and suffering!'

He glared at me as if I'd personally driven the bulldozer. I made a sour face and looked uneasily through the stone columns and the thickening mist beyond.

'Look,' I said. 'I don't know about the Folk. But sometimes, late at night, you can hear hundreds of trotters running along the road, rooting around the Hëlweed, and when I get up again the next morning, the Hëlweed that was creeping towards our house has been torn up. I think the ghost pigs are the only things keeping the Hëlweed away from us.'

Helen and Derek were staring at me. Oh, right, like these two hadn't admitted to believing in the Wee People!

'Mulkytine himself probably leads them in their war with the Helweed!' said Helen dramatically. 'Ooh, this is a very spooky place.'

'Don't say his name, he might hear you,' I muttered, and in the fog it was easy to think he might be out there somewhere, listening.

'It's a miserable hole, is what it is,' growled Derek.

'Where we goin', anyway? There's no cows in here. I thought we were gettin' a cow?'

'He's right you know, Brian,' said Helen. 'I don't see any cows down here.'

I sighed.

'This way,' I said, and we plunged into the fog.

4.

MULKYTINE

THE FOG THAT enveloped Ghost Pig Estate was no ordinary fog. Eyes stinging, skin prickling, throat sore, nose numb, I waved my arms as if swimming or drowning. We should have had gas masks. Mum had been giving us stickers when she should have been giving us bio-hazard suits.

The builders had very thoughtfully left piles of rubble and rubbish everywhere. Lots of twisted metal and rusty nails and huge heaps of broken bricks covered in weeds and occupied by cunning clans of feral rats.

The solid, lumpy shapes of empty houses swamped with Hëlweed loomed around us as we threaded our way through the maze of the estate. The road became worse, the Hëlweed thicker and the houses more decrepit. I carefully guided Helen and Derek around the weed-covered pothole next to our house. I didn't get on with them but I wasn't going to let them fall into that dark and evil pit.

I peered around, squinting. This would have been perfectly simple without the fog. As it was, we could end up wandering in circles in this muck for hours if we weren't careful, and sooner or later one of us would slip and fall into a flooded pothole.

'There,' I said. A low, wide shadow ahead. Was that the shore of the Pond? I pointed so the others could see, and led the way. Somewhere out there was the Isle of Lisashee and the Tower of Long Lisa.

'Thank goodness,' Helen tried to say without choking.

We blundered forward until I felt grass underfoot. Ah, we'd found it!

Just then, something squealed. Something prehistoric and savage and angry.

We froze. I didn't have much hair on my head, but it all crawled like a nest of spiders.

'Is it a dragon?' said Helen, almost sounding hopeful. 'That sounded like a dragon!'

'Dragon, me eye!' said Derek. 'That was a rhinoceros!'

A black shape surged out of the mist.

We screamed.

Derek threw a rock. It bounced off the monster's hide. Helen held up both hands in a calming gesture and made squeaky piggy noises. I screamed again, grabbed them each by an arm and ran blindly for a few yards, then stopped, with nothing but mud in front of us. I could still hear the trample of hooves and a heavy huff of breath behind me, but when I turned to look, the mist had swallowed up the shape once more.

Was . . . was that Mulkytine?

Mulkytine, the legendary boar of Lisashee? Who had escaped from the Otherworld to wreak havoc in seven counties? Who had rampaged across the hills, bogs and fields for centuries? No, no, he couldn't be real. *He couldn't.* Some of those escaped pigs had survived and bred in the wild, that was all. They'd gone feral and now, possibly, craved the flesh of human children. Ok, fine. This was fine.

'What *was* that?' said Derek. 'Where'd it go? I want to go home!'

'Everybody stay calm,' said Helen, her voice shaking. 'EVERYBODY STAY CALM!'

I stared around wildly. And then I thought I saw movement in the fog.

'There it is!' I hissed. 'This way! Stay together!'

We ran along the shore, away from the looming shape. There was nowhere to hide, no cover to creep behind. There was the fog, but I couldn't help but feel that it was hiding Mulkytine from us rather than us from Mulkytine. Maybe the library? No, that was the *other* direction!

'That way!' I pointed. I could see a long, flat shape laid out across the mud ahead of us. I knew what that was. 'Come on!'

Derek and Helen followed. A terrible squeal erupted from somewhere beside us. Derek and Helen passed me at a dead sprint.

There were old wooden poles stuck into the grass and mud, groping for the sky at various distressing angles. This was where the old ferry used to dock. The ferry itself had been eaten by the mud long ago, but someone had since laid long wide boards down on the surface of the Pond, creating a dry path all the way out to the island. You had to walk along carefully, balancing, while the mud squelched underneath. It didn't look safe and it didn't look easy, and the only reason it was there was so someone could go fetch the cow for the Festival. Usually, I loved it. Crossing to the island on those wooden boards was the most fun I had every year. Not this time.

Helen and Derek had sprinted past the rotting dock. I yelled at them to come back and follow me, and hit the boards running, which is not what those boards were designed for. They slipped and slid and moved underfoot. I couldn't watch where I was stepping because I was going sideways, looking back at Helen and Derek who were teetering behind me. They had their arms out straight, tilting up and down as if they were playing airplanes.

'What are we doing?' wailed Helen.

'We're followin' that fool!' roared Derek.

We reached the end of the first plank and hopped across the space to the second. Derek was last, and as he landed a thunderous snort tore through the fog from the direction of the shore. Something landed heavily on the far end of the first board, and the end near us shot into the air, spraying mud everywhere. Then it slapped back down again and we heard hooves clattering, getting louder.

'It's following us?' I gasped in disbelief. 'It's following us! Keep going!'

There was mud underneath us, fog around us and above us, a monster behind us and only a thin strip of dirty, slippery wood in front, a straight and narrow path we could not stray from. It's hard to run in a stinking fog at the best of times. We weren't really running so much as shuffling rapidly, hopping from one board to the next, peering into the grey blank haze, searching for some sign of the Isle of Lisashee.

'There!' I pointed at a dark patch in the fog, more in hope than certainty. 'It's the island!'

Mulkytine squealed. We stopped shuffling and just ran, slipping, falling, our arms windmilling, our feet going out from under us. I lost my balance and skated along the slippery wet wood on one foot. I got my second foot down and skated along some more, nice and smooth, like crossing an iced-over puddle. Then I hit a bad patch and was thrown forward. I rolled once along the board and landed in something soft and crackly and sharp. Thorns tore at my clothes and stabbed my back and legs. I ripped myself away, stumbled to my feet and reached out, pulling Helen and Derek ashore. Then I stooped down and lifted the end of the board out of the sucking mud and flung it away from the shore as far as I could, which wasn't very far.

A hedge of thorns blocked our way and I could see no path through. Mulkytine the boar came clattering out of the fog and slid along the board. He looked across at us. The fog cleared briefly and I saw two huge jagged tusks, two beady eyes, two sharp ears and a great tuft of bristles and spines along his back, a huge powerful bulk of muscle and fat.

'Ha ha,' I said in a shrill, high-pitched voice. 'The boar aboard the board.'

Helen and Derek glared at me.

Mulkytine reached the end of the board and lowered his

great snout to sniff at the mud. He squealed, and waded in. The mud came up to his flanks, but he pushed through like an ice-breaker cutting across a frozen ocean.

'Aw, leave it out,' muttered Derek.

'We need an escape route,' said Helen with surprising calm, and she looked around at the wall of thorns which surrounded us on all sides save the lake shore with its approaching monster.

'There's no escape route,' she reported. 'We shall have to make friends with it.'

'Make friends with *that*?' Derek said, pointing at Mulkytine, who was swimming closer, pushing a wave of mud ahead of him, leaving a spreading wake behind. 'Does that look like it wants to make friends?'

I grabbed Helen's arm and pulled her back. We retreated slowly to the wall of thorns as Mulkytine clambered ashore. The giant boar glared at us, shook the mud from his body, lowered his head, tusks jagged and sharp and fur badly in need of a brushing.

'Look, I'm sorry guys,' I said. 'This has never happened before . . .'

Mulkytine charged.

Something white and glowing pushed its way out from the thorns, and the smooth, snowy flanks of a large, serene and beautiful white cow stepped between us and Mulkytine. The cow lowed gently. The boar snorted and shook its head, then reluctantly turned and slipped back into the mud and mist.

The cow swung its head, perched on a neck as graceful as any swan's, and looked at the Junior Action (Cow Fetching)

Sub Group with eyes that were big and brown and full of kind amusement. She tilted her head in invitation and somehow it just seemed obvious what she wanted us to do. As if in a slow and heavy dream, we walked up to her and one by one climbed onto her back. When we were settled she set out across the lake. Her steps were slow and precise, as careful as a dancer's, and each hoof sank barely a half-inch into the mud.

Helen and Derek were wide-eyed and dazeed, but I had done this twice before, without the boar, and somehow, for some reason, it had never struck me as strange or odd or magical. That was the thing about Knockmealldown, curse or no curse. When something like that happened, when you rode on the back of a beautiful, wise cow across the mud and back to the Green, you didn't really question it, though some part of you wondered why you weren't questioning it, and later you just accepted that it had happened.

'Told you we wouldn't need a rope,' I said.

5.

THE COMMITTEE ON THE GREEN

LOOKING BACK AT everything that happened later it might seem odd, but crossing the Mud Pond through the fog on the back of the cow was the most dream-like moment of the whole Festival. Mulkytine's squeals fading in the distance, the stink and the Smell, the nasty gloop of the mud, the grey of the fog – none of it seemed to matter. We weren't scared or embarrassed or uncomfortable; we just swayed gently with each step and felt safe.

When the cow stepped onto the shore of the Pond we blinked as if waking up, and slid off. She went to stand on the tiny strip of grass that was all that remained of the Green, gave a slight shake of her head, and began to graze.

'Her name's Lackley,' I said, shivering in the weird after-shock of being chased by a pig and saved by a cow.

'We know what her name is, Brian,' said Helen. 'We all know the Legend.'

Of course they did. Knockmealldown had more legends and stories and tales than most villages had doors and windows, and everybody knew them. There was a city under the lake, there was a legendary bandit queen, there was the ferocious Mulkytine, there were the banshees and the mischievous Cluaracan. Wild hunts in the sky, strange fortunes hidden under doorways, people stolen away and rescued or never seen again, heroes who slept fearlessly in graveyards chasing off monsters looking to steal recently-deceased bodies, arguments between bards and cats, wicked people who were punished, good people who were rewarded, rogues who prospered and good people who suffered. So many stories you couldn't keep track of them all.

Most important of all was the story of the Great Festival. It all started when a local chief invited the King and Queen of the Other Folk to a feast. He set his daughter to baking the bread, but she wasn't a very good baker and ended up burning the whole batch. Scared of how much trouble she'd be in, she ran away, accompanied by a cow named Lackley, and had lots of odd adventures. She gave her last scrap of food to a tiny starving man she met at the side of the road, and in return he taught her a secret recipe for special bread and told her to go home.

When she got back, no time at all had passed, so she made the bread using the secret recipe. When her father tasted the results it was so horrible he was furious, but Lackley the cow told him to serve it to the Good Folk. The Gentry enjoyed the bread so much they rewarded the chief and his daughter with riches and blessings, and it turned out – PLOT TWIST! – the tiny starving man had been the King in disguise all along. After that, the legend goes, the Good Folk came back to Knockmealldown for a Great Festival every hundred years.

Obviously it wasn't the same cow. Obviously it was a *different* beautiful, wise cow that lived on an island in the middle of the lake and could calm a huge scary boar that OBVIOUSLY wasn't the ferocious Mulkytine. Obviously.

We sat ourselves down not far from the cow and watched her for a while. She was beautiful, from the tip of her curling horns, to her elegant hooves to her slender tail. There wasn't a speck of mud on her, either, even after crossing the Pond with three kids on her back. Watching her, we seemed to have no worries, no fears, no discomforts. The Smell didn't seem as Smelly. The fog didn't seem as foggy. Knockmealldown didn't seem as Knockmealldowny.

'She's a beautiful animal,' said Helen.

'Aye, she's a queen among cows,' said Derek.

She seemed to glow, and glow brighter. Light filled the fog all around us. A curlew called from across the mud.

'What is that?' said Helen.

'It's magic!' said Derek, leaping to his feet. 'They *are* comin'! The Little People *are* comin'!'

'I think it's just the sun,' I said, though in Knockmealldown the sun appearing *is* a kind of magic.

'What? Get out,' said Derek. 'No way. Where do you think we are? It's more likely to be the Little People.'

The fog thinned and faded. A shining disc appeared in the sky, growing brighter and hotter, turning yellow as it burned through the last dregs of mist. Helen was blinking away tears. I had to stop myself staring directly at the light. What was it called again? Oh, yeah! The sun. It was just that it had been so long. And the sky is blue! I'd nearly forgotten.

'That's always a sure sign that it's goin' to rain,' said Derek, spitting into the mud. 'When you see the sun shinin' like that.'

Lackley serenely chewed her grass.

'Did you know, there used to be a crannog here?' Helen said as we watched the sunlight glimmer on the mud.

'Yes,' Derek and me said together.

Bob Bellamore's battered old 4x4 came bouncing around the Hëlweed Houses and pulled up. Bob, Sheila, Mum and Dad piled out, blinking, dazzled by the light, and uncomfortably hot in their heavy Knockmealldown summer clothes.

'Nearly drove into the Pond with that sun in me eyes,' said Bob.

'I hope this doesn't keep people inside for the Festival,' said Sheila, sounding worried. 'It's so bright and they might all get sunburned. They're not used to it, you know.'

'Do you really think so?' said Mum, shielding her eyes and looking around and trying not to sound too hopeful.

'Don't worry about any of that,' said Bob, grinning. 'There'll be no shortage of punters out and about tomorrow, I guarantee you that!'

He put his hands on his hips, thrust out his chest and took a deep, invigorating breath of sunshine. Then he coughed and hacked a bit, because the Smell and the Estate hadn't gone away, you know.

'I suppose you're right,' said Sheila, smiling hopefully.

'Let's hope so,' said Mum insincerly. 'Hey, I see you

guys got the cow! Good work! Now come on, we've got to get the marquee up while the sun's still shining.'

Dad already had the bulky length of the marquee halfway out of the back of the 4x4 and was slowly bending backwards under the weight.

'It's all right!' he called in a strained voice. 'I've got it! No problem!'

We rushed to save his spine, carried the marquee across the Green to the designated Marquee Spot and unpacked it, spreading the canvas and connecting various poles, catching our fingers in bits that moved and unfolded unpredictably. We pulled the canvas over the frame. Derek got tangled up in the guy lines and dropped the mallet on his foot.

'Here, let me,' said Helen, and she picked it up and began hammering a peg into the ground.

'Gimme that!' said Derek, grabbing at the mallet as Helen swung it past his ear. He swore. Helen turned on him indignantly. I went over to keep the peace. Our antics were observed by Lackley and by a growing crowd of locals, who only rarely braved the traps and terrors of the Estate. They were mainly there to say hello to the cow, but they were kind enough to give advice on what we were doing wrong. The kids in the crowd divided up into two groups centered around the figures of Tom Tracey and Tricia Mulligan.

At last the marquee was erected and everyone went over to admire Lackley. Mum and Dad and me sat on the grass and watched the sunlight sparkling on the mud. It was lovely – but I kept a lookout for a lurking Mulkytine.

'Are you all right?' said Dad. 'You seem a bit shaken.'

'No, I'm fine,' I said. 'Well, I mean, I think there was some sort of . . . wild pig running around. It gave us a fright and we nearly fell in the Pond.'

'A *what*?' said Mum, alarmed. 'Am I going to have to call animal control or something?'

'Maybe,' I said, uncertainly. Now I was wondering if the panic and the fog had made a monster out of a guinea pig. It didn't seem as terrifying sitting there, basking in the rare warmth. 'Nah,' I heard myself saying. 'It was nothing, really.'

'It doesn't feel so bad, does it, when the sun comes out?' said Dad. He was right. Everything seemed bright and calm and warm and beautiful. Fields were glowing in shades of green, and the leaves on the trees were basking like sunbathers. Mist still clung to the houses of the Ghost Pig Estate, but Knockmealldown itself seemed like a lizard whose skin was about to crack and flake and shrivel away, leaving something new and clean and young behind.

Listen to me. Five minutes of direct sunlight and I was already going daft.

'I think it only happens once every hundred years,' I said.

'The day the sun shines forever,' Mum said.

'All the flowers bloom, all the birds sing,' said Dad. 'And people search frantically for their swimwear so they can go out and get a nice healthy sunburn.'

'Maybe this time it'll be different,' Mum said wistfully. 'Maybe this time the Festival will be a good one.'

'Like in the legend,' said Dad. 'Like they used to be. And maybe will be again . . .'

Oh, yes. The good old days when the Knockmealldown Festival was the best in the world rather than the worst. Why were they the best? Nobody could really say. What used to happen at these Festivals? Nobody could remember. When was it that these Festivals were so great? Back before they built the pig factory, they said.

Dad's family were from the village, and it was in part because of his fuzzy memories of glorious golden summer Festivals that he'd persuaded us to move back. As far as I was concerned it was just another daft Knockmealldown story.

He sounded wistful and guilty. I didn't say: 'It'll take more than a few sunny days to make up for the last three years,' but I didn't have to. They could feel my scepticism coming out of me like invisible rays of heat from the sun.

It was Sheila who noticed we'd put the canvas on the frame of the marquee inside out, much to the hilarity of Mulligans and Traceys. They competed with each other to laugh the loudest and make the most cutting remarks until Tricia Mulligan did a quick switch and began defending us against the cruel lazy ditch-hurlers led by Tom Tracey. Soon they forgot about us and were busy snarling at each other while we laboriously pulled the canvas off.

Nobody noticed the sky go dark, or felt the wind rise. A sudden gust flattened the grass on the Green and made the canvas billow. The feuding groups paused and looked upwards.

Lackley was nowhere to be seen.

'The marquee!' screamed Mum. 'Grab hold!'

Everyone grabbed hold of some canvas or a pole or a guy line. A wall of wind and rain moving faster than most speeding bullets walloped into the marquee and all the Junior and Senior members of the Knockmealldown Festival Committee clinging to it. The canvas took off like a kite and lifted us off the ground, carrying me, Mum, Dad, Derek, Helen, Bob and Sheila across the Green and dropping us into the Pond.

The squall of wind and rain stopped as suddenly as it'd started.

Both Mulligans and Traceys, soaked and shocked, stared at us in silence as we clambered out, caked in mud. The marquee sank into the black sticky depths. I couldn't tell one committee member from the next until Helen burst into tears and stomped off, flinging mud from herself in great thick handfuls.

'I'm going home!' she said. 'And I'm not coming back to your stupid useless Festival!'

'Ah no!' Bob called after her. 'It'll be fine! Tomorrow everything'll be grand! It's going to be a Great Festival!'

Helen shouted something back at him. I couldn't hear what it was because of the mud in my ears, which was probably just as well.

Lackley the cow wandered slowly back onto the Green, and recommenced eating. The sun was no longer shining. It looked like it was going to rain again soon. Derek spat on the ground.

'Told ya,' he said.

Part Two:
Saturday

1.

THE OPENING

I WAS ON a rickety little podium next to the Pond – basically a strip of board laid across a pile of pallets – trying to set up the sound system without getting electrocuted. Under the heavy clouds above, nighttime was hanging around like a cheeky teenager who won't go home even though the chipper's closed, and the heavens were getting ready to fall. The first day of the Festival was set to be a typical summer's day in Knockmealldown, with rain as thick as a tropical jungle.

Mum was studying the clouds and the haze of drizzle approaching across the nearby fields, looking both depressed and oppressed.

'It's going to rain, isn't it?' she said. We both glanced at the Mud Pond. Under the gloop, Mum's borrowed marquee was sinking towards the centre of the earth.

I'd managed to get myself wrapped in the cords and wires of the sound system while Dad fiddled furiously with the soundboard and the microphone. The speakers screamed and howled with feedback every time I moved. The electronic screeching was giving Dad a splitting headache, and he was trembling too much to actually do anything with his screwdriver. He winced with pain at every howl.

We had dug the sound system out from under the stage of the Parish Hall. It was damp, covered in cobwebs and mouse droppings, and littered with a small pile of mummified bats. I'd spent the last hour trying to clean and untangle the cables.

'Think you nearly got it that time,' said Derek from the safety of the grass, chewing on a breakfast roll. He was trying to keep a safe distance between himself and an auld fella in a terrible coat and a terrible hat who had turned up out of nowhere and started tuning a fiddle as old and battered as himself. A length of blue twine knotted raggedly around the auld fella's waist was attached to a tiny creature that might have been a rat or a dog. It was sitting in the grass and scratching itself vigorously. The same auld fella and dog turned up out of nowhere at every Festival and played grating, awful tunes all weekend. People tried to give him money, but he just wouldn't go away.

A piercing scream came from the speakers, driving nails into my skull. Dad dropped the screwdriver, crawled off the podium and curled up on the grass. Mum patted his shoulder gently. When my head stopped ringing I heard Mum say, 'What on earth are they doing?'

She was pointing at a crowd of villagers moving through the Estate. We heard voices raised, laughing and chatting, then coughing and hacking whenever they went through particularly thick pockets of Smell. They were stepping gingerly over the rutted road, buttoning up their coats, milling together, and making their way to the Green.

Derek giggled.

'Maybe they're comin' to the Festival Opening!'

Then he stopped giggling and stared in horror with the rest of us. What if he were right? What if all these people werre coming to the Opening? Nobody ever came to the Opening! Did they actually think the Folk were going to turn up? All we had was a scrap of wood for a podium and a spaghetti-monster mess of a sound system. Wasn't it humiliating enough without people actually turning up to witness it?

In the growing light the people tried to swarm onto the Green. They spread along the shore and stood together on the road.

Still draped in the sound system, I went and stood beside Mum and Dad, staring at the lively, chattering, expectant crowd, yanking at the plug to get it out of the extension cord and cut off the low, irritating hum. The plug wouldn't budge. Dad absentmindedly handed me a microphone, and I nearly overbalanced and rolled into the Pond.

Lackley the cow momentarily paused in her ruminative chewing, swung her head gracefully towards the small thing at the end of the length of blue twine, and as clear as day, I swear to God, I heard her say: 'Oh my goodness. Has it really been a hundred years already? I'd quite lost track.'

The little thing wagged a tiny stump of a tail, and replied, 'It goes by so fast, doesn't it?'

'They just talked,' I said into the microphone. My voice huffed out of the speakers on either side of the stage. 'The cow and the dog just talked.'

'Give 'em the mike!' someone called. 'Maybe they'll give us a song!'

Lackley looked at the dog and the dog looked at Lackley, then they both looked up at me and shook their heads. The crowd was too busy laughing to notice, and then they stopped laughing because there was a sudden horrible, ear-shredding wail. Except it wasn't the sound system. The auld fella with the dog was drawing his bow across the strings of his fiddle.

The crowd seemed to curl up in on itself as everyone stopped talking and blocked their ears. Then the old man looked down at the dog, and the dog gave the old man a nod, and the auld fella began to play.

A note as pure as crystal and light as a dandelion seed rose, and all eyes rose to follow it. The clouds over Knockmealldown broke apart, revealing a dawn sky as sweet and innocent as a gurgling baby. Morning sun cast a sparkling light over the Green, and suddenly we were all trailing shadows like fragile cloaks made of cobwebs and wishes.

The crowd, which had been muttering, hushed as if every man, woman and child was holding their breath. And into the expectant silence, came a rising *clip-clop, clip-clop*. The crowd parted to let a pony and rider through. The rider seemed to be made of mud, except for the eyes, which were wide and furious. The pony, which was spotless and seemed to be in charge, came to a stop next to the podium.

'Could someone please tell me what is going on here?' demanded the rider.

'Helen?' I said, confused. Hadn't she left yesterday, also covered in mud?

'Can I get down now?' she asked. 'Would that be all right? Do I have your permission to dismount?'

'Uh,' I said.

'Certainly,' said the horse. Helen slid off and mounted the podium with what dignity she could muster.

'You look ridiculous,' she told me, wiping muck off her face. 'I've had a very peculiar morning.'

'Ah Helen,' Derek said. 'You didn't have to dress up special. What's that perfume you've on? Eau de cow?'

'Excuse me?' said Lackley. Derek jumped.

'Quiet, you yob,' said Helen regally. A shockingly deep and angry growl came from the little dog, and everyone shut up. Except the auld fella. The auld fella kept playing. He hopped lightly on his feet, and twirled, and whirled, and danced.

An electric thrill ran right through me. Every hair on my body stood up, and light cool fingers seemed to run gently up and down my spine. Over the music I heard a strange sound coming from somewhere behind me, a rushing and a trilling and a multitude of flutterings. Every face in the crowd stared at us. Not at us; *behind* us. I turned, wrapping the cords and cables tighter around me but not really caring. I didn't really care about anything else just then. Neither did anybody else. Everybody was looking across the Pond.

Something was happening on the Isle of Lisashee.

2.

THE FOLK

SOMETHING WAS HAPPENING. Something complicated and confusing. The island was alive with movement and colour, movement and colour that was accumulating, gathering together, building up and then

colours

exploding

skyward

birds

a firework made of birds.

Hundreds of them, thousands of them, a massive flock spreading across the sky over the lake and sweeping down towards the shore and the Green. As far as I could tell they were all perfectly ordinary birds, but of every type. I didn't see any bigger than a crow or a magpie, and the rest were a bewildering variety of robins and thrushes and starlings and swifts and swallows. They all flew down and shot over the crowd and then back around the lake, a huge fluttering, flapping mob. They swept around the lake and back and then twice more, and every eye followed them in utter fascination, and out of the corner of every eye something began to happen on the lake, something that started at the Isle and spread out across the mud, like a mist pulling back to reveal something that had been there all along.

The birds flew over us one more time and then shot high into the sky and spread out, flying off in all directions, shrinking until they were tiny black dots, and then they were gone, and all eyes returned to the lake where the last scraps of morning mist were fading and this new thing that was somehow as old as stone was waiting to be seen.

Platforms and bridges, walkways and arches, trellises and stairways, all sparkling clean and white in the sun, even though it came out of the muck. All made of wood, carved and smoothed and polished. A whole intricate, elaborate series of structures that stretched out over the Pond, linked with bridges, some covered, some open, all converging on the Isle at the centre of the lake and rising to surround the Tower of Long Lisa, now hung with sheets of coloured cloth, with walls and stairs and balconies.

And out of the Tower, crossing onto the largest walkway which ran straight to the shore, came the Other Crowd, the Gentle Folk, the Little People – but Little People big and small.

I was amazement. I was disbelief. I was wonder.

Most were small, like children, but with beards and wizened faces. Some were tiny, and they had wings on their backs and their bodies were covered in blue tattoos and their hair was spiked and they wore swords and spears and looked fierce and dangerous. Of the ones who were more or less normal size, some were perfectly human in appearance, except you knew when you looked at them that they weren't, though you weren't quite sure how you knew. When it came to the rest, there wasn't much doubt. Skin-colours ranged from polished ebony black to beautiful bright yellow, to shimmering green, to sky blue, to a white so white it glowed. Many had skin that wasn't technically skin but bark or stone or moss, and others had fur of various types, or were covered in spikes and thorns and leaves and earth.

Horns sprouted from their heads; tiny little nubbins that were round and smooth and adorable, or huge racks of interlocking antlers that seemed to rise high enough to pose a hazard to low-flying planes. Some were more animal than human, with goats' feet or herons' heads or tusks or snouts or whiskers or all of the above. Some were lumpy, dumpy and squat; some were thinner than ropes. Some had pointy teeth and long claws and hungry looks.

They weren't beautiful, exactly, not the way the people in Una's magazines were beautiful. They were *interesting* to look at; fascinating. Like complicated bits of scenery that winked and talked back at you. They were more real than everything else, somehow, as if they had put themselves together out of pieces of the world, bits of land and sky.

The shocked human crowd drew back fearfully, respectfully, and allowed them to fill the Green. The Folk were very still and very silent, until they parted like water, and their King and Queen approached the podium.

They stepped lightly, delicately, never seeming to touch the ground. They were slender and graceful, and though the horns made them seem tall, their crowned heads only came up as high as myself. Their skin glowed pale and white, with a hint of green, and their faces were as sharp as hatchets. Their eyes were wide and never blinked, and had a look of childish innocence to them. Their hair was long and reddish-yellow, tied up in elaborate braids and ponytails with rings of carved gold. Their clothes were made of leather and velvet and silk, dyed many colours. Leaves and berries and garlands of flowers and ivy were woven through their hair and clothes. Two small, blunt horns grew from the Queen's forehead, and two large antlers grew from the sides of the King's head. They looked back at us but they were not smiling.

'I don't believe it,' I said. I'd completely forgotten that I was still holding the microphone. My voice came blaring out of the speakers in crisp, clear stereo. 'It's the *fairies*.'

3.

THE FLOATING PALACE

AS SOON AS I said it I knew I'd made a dreadful mistake.

The King and Queen's eyes widened in shock and their lips went thin with offense. There was a gasp from the human crowd. I heard Derek swear and Bob moan.

'You utter twit, Brian, not the *f* word!' said Helen. 'It's terribly bad manners to call them by that name!'

I gave her a look that was half glare and half *please-get-me-out-of-this.*

'I'm sorry!' I said, still speaking into the mike. 'I forgot! I didn't mean to! I'm so sorry!'

Dad quickly snatched the mike away and Mum put a hand on my shoulder to shut me up.

'I'm sorry,' I said to them. 'I'm *really* sorry!'

The King and the Queen had stopped. They looked like two people who had run out of a short supply of patience and were about to start using up their endless reserves of rage.

'My Lord, my Lady!' The voice seemed to bound jauntily out of the crowd of Folk, followed by the speaker himself. 'If it pleases you, do mount the stage and make your proclamations! Let your hearts be lightened and your troubles relieved by the entertainments of the Great Festival.'

Portly and round, like a party balloon with legs, the gentleman had a small hat perched jauntily on his head and a face red and raw from sun and wind. He was wearing old-fashioned but aristocratic clothes of brown tweed. A blackthorn stick hung rakishly from one hand. He fussed cheerfully around the King and Queen, urging them on with bows, gestures and waving hands. The King lowered his head so his chin rested on his chest and the Queen rolled her eyes, but there were faint, frosty smiles on their lips.

A little ball of soot shot out of the crowd of Other Folk and bounced along the ground. The portly gentleman gave a yell of annoyance and kicked it like a football. It flew straight at my head, too fast for me to duck or do anything other than utter a quick 'meep'. Darkness and feathers engulfed me. I staggered backwards and choked as the microphone wires round my neck tightened. I blindly struggled, twisted and pulled, but all I managed to do was get myself in a worse tangle. Squeaking with rage and frustration, the ball of soot still all over my face, I toppled over and fell off the podium.

The King and Queen were like pins in a bowling alley. I rolled straight at them, and would have squashed them flat or sent them flying, possibly into the lake or perhaps even into next week, if they hadn't spread their arms, sprouted feathers and floated into the air above us, hovering there for a moment while I rolled helplessly beneath. The whole thing happened in a second, as smooth, elegant and beautiful as an acrobatic display.

The ball of soot grew two hands, which it used to cling to my head, and two feet, which it planted into the ground to bring us skidding to a stop inches from the shore of the lake. The royal pair settled back down onto the ground and a strange blue glow surrounded them. Their eyes darkened and flashed like storm clouds full of lightning. Their teeth sharpened, talons sprung from their hands. They seemed to fall towards me, the horns on their foreheads savage and wild, the ivy in their hair writhing and full of thorns.

The soot-thing climbed onto my chest with clawed yellow feet and stared down at me with eyes that were nothing but pitch-black holes. It wore a ragged dress of some sort of rough, coarse material, completely unlike anything the rest of the Other Folk were wearing. It had a nose or a beak – it could have been either – that was a long, yellow stalk. Under the nose something shifted, like a tiny maelstrom on a dark sea, whirling round and round, drawing me down, drowning me.

The King and Queen stopped, and blinked, as if confused.

'Ooooooooh Mammy, oh Daddy – you never said they'd be ugly!' squeaked the thing on my chest. 'So strange! Strange and deformed and stupid! You can tell how stupid they are by the face on 'em, as if they'd never seen a beautiful maid of the Good Folk before in their short and miserable lives! But sort of cute, too. Like pups! May I have this one for a pet?'

None of the other Folk seemed to notice the creature,

except for the portly gentleman, who came sweeping down and caught the raggedy thing by the scruff of the neck, pulled it off my chest and threw it to the ground. He stooped over the little heap of soot and feathers and growled at it in a low voice.

'Off the boy, Fester, off the boy! None of your discourtesy or half-witted tricks, girl!'

He gently but firmly pulled me free of the wires and cables and stood me upright. I only had eyes for the King and Queen, bracing myself for claws and teeth, talons and horns, but the transformation had passed, and now they were back to their previous state, their faces angry, offended and bewildered.

'If you value your life, sir,' murmured the gentleman, brushing dust and dirt from my clothes, 'stand over there and neither move nor speak. For the rest of the Festival, if you can manage it. Like oil on burning waters, so you are.'

He turned to the King and Queen and waved his arms in wide gestures that seemed to take in the whole world.

'Oh dear, my lord, my lady, this is an inauspicious start! Please pretend that never happened! Forgive the foolish clumsy child! He is just a weakling, and no doubt simple in the head, to boot!'

'The simple-minded have better manners,' said the King with a snarl. 'The simple-minded see things more clearly than the clever. This one thinks he is clever.'

'Clever enough to seek to lay hands on us,' said the Queen. 'Not in a thousand years has anyone been so *clever*. Not in a thousand years have we had to wear our wild and ancient forms. This cannot be tolerated.'

'Well, your majesties have been under a lot of stress lately. Perhaps we can postpone judgment on the boy until the business at hand has been completed?'

He made a sweeping gesture towards the podium where the Festival Committee waited, anxious and horrified. The faces of the crowd were twisted into expressions of excruciating embarrassment and shocked amazement. Now that I was no longer in immediate danger of being royally eviscerated, I was utterly mortified. I couldn't look anyone in the eye. My skin crawled, my ears burned and my stomach sank down deeper than the dinosaurs at the bottom of the Mud Pond.

'After these insults and assaults?' said the King after a moment. My stomach plunged deeper still. 'We will retire to the Floating Palace. Bring the wretches responsible for this calamity to us directly.'

The crowd groaned. Bob closed his eyes and rubbed his forehead. Sheila pursed her lips and glared at me. I'd never seen mild-tempered Sheila get angry about anything before, but she was furious now. Mum and Dad were frozen, like pale statues. Helen stared at me through a mask of mud and Derek had a face on him of utter contempt.

The King and the Queen turned, their scarlet cloaks swirling from their shoulders, shining like silk in the morning sun, and proceeded back across the walkway. Their subjects followed, darting glances back at us, some angry, some concerned, some pitying. I couldn't bear to watch the Other Folk go; I couldn't bear to look at the dismayed crowd of humans. So instead I bent over the puddle of feathers and rags lying almost flat in the grass.

'Hello?' I said, trying to work out exactly where the face was supposed to be. 'Fester, is it? Are you okay?'

The thin yellow beak unfolded and a pair of black shadows blinked. Clumps of scruffy feathers poked through ripped and torn rags.

'A hat,' said the squeaky little voice. 'If I only had a hat, I might get some respect. One with a feather in it, don't you think?'

'You already have lots of feathers,' I pointed out, slumping cross-legged on the ground beside her.

'Sorry you got kicked,' I added, and held out a hand.

Fester hesitated, then unfolded a wing, which I gripped, pulling her up until she was sitting. She weighed only a feather or two more than nothing and barely came up to my shoulders.

'Never mind, it was nothing,' she said. 'The Cluaracan has to show me who's boss or I forget meself. To be honest I'm not used to others being able to see me and talk to me. Are you sure you're able to see me and talk to me? You're not pretending to see me and talk to me for a joke?'

'No,' I said. 'I can see you and talk to you. Er, can't everyone?'

'No, not so much. Well how about that? Humans can see me and talk to me! What an interesting development! Aren't you the freindly one!'

'Am I?' I said glumly. 'I've made a mess of everything. I insulted you using the *f* word, didn't I? I nearly ran over the King and Queen. I just can't believe this is happening. The stories are actually true! Fai— Other Folk are real! There

53

was going to be a Great Festival! Everything was going to be okay! And I ruined it. Mum and Dad will kill me.'

'Ah don't be so hard on yourself,' said Fester. 'You're only a thick ignorant human child who doesn't know any better. Listen to me, now, and listen well. Their Royal Highnesses were already on the warpath! They've been in a bad mood over the state of Knockmealldown for years! They were all set to give you lot a piece of their mind for building filthy old pig factories and shabby old housing estates right up against their lake! The insult of it! Oh they were furious. They were going to give you a chance to explain yourselves and then decide whether or not to turn you into birds for the rest of your lives. So none of that's just your fault, to be sure.'

'Oh,' I said. 'Well, that's good to know.'

'You just made everything worse, that's all,' she said. 'They were expecting all sorts of grovelling and apologising and begging on bended knees and offers of wealth and favours. Instead they got you.'

'Oh no,' I moaned, burying my head in my hands. 'This can't be happening.'

Striding across the Green came the portly little man in the brown coat, smiling affably. The Cluaracan.

'Fester, stop bothering the poor boy,' he said. 'He has enough worries on his youthful shoulders without your confusing nonsense.' He turned to me. 'Don't listen to a word that creature says. She's madder than a barrel of turnips, even for one of the Good Folk. I'm the Cluaracan. You must be Brian. You'd better come with me, and bring the rest of your friends and relatives, too. Don't worry! We'll get all this cleared up in no time, and soon be celebrating the Great Festival just as we did in the old days!'

I looked at him gratefully and stood up. This guy seemed to know what he was doing, and he also seemed to be on our side. I had to hope he'd smooth everything over and get things back on track. Bob, Sheila, Mum, Dad, Helen and Derek all climbed down off the podium and we followed the Cluaracan out onto the Pond.

'What is that?' said Dad, sounding dazed. He waved his hand around in an effort to take in the beautiful, intricate white structure that was now resting lightly on the waters of the lake. 'I've never seen anything like it.'

'That?' said the Cluaracan offhandedly. 'Oh, it's just the Floating Palace, our traditional residence during the Great Festival. Normally Knockmealldowners are welcome to come and go as they please – but perhaps we'll let things thaw out a bit first.'

'Brian didn't mean any harm, you know,' said Mum. 'You're not going to let them do anything to him, are you? That wouldn't be fair. It was clearly an accident.'

'Of course!' said the Cluaracan. 'Just as you *accidentally* built factories and houses all over our land! Not to worry! We'll get it straightened out!'

His tone of voice was reassuring, but somehow his words were not. I shivered as if I was back in yesterday's fog, with Mulkytine's terrible squeals getting louder.

The railings of the boardwalks were carved into circles and spirals and polished so they gleamed and were smooth to the touch.

'It's very beautiful,' said Helen, while Derek stamped

hard on the boards as though expecting them to melt back into the Pond at any moment.

'You're some flippin' *eejit*,' he said to me.

'I know,' I said miserably.

'You were very undiplomatic,' said Helen.

'Very,' I agreed, close to tears. I stole a glance at Mum and Dad, but they were walking stiffly and robotically, as if still in shock. 'I'm sorry,' I mumbled. 'I didn't mean . . . I never thought . . .'

'Ah leave him alone, lads,' said Fester, waddling beside me with her ungainly feet and her mismatched wings. 'It could happen to a bishop.'

'What the jaypers is that thing, anyway?' said Derek. 'It looks like a crow and a pigeon got stuck in a blender.'

'That's Fester,' I said, my voice faint and raw and hot from shame. 'Er, Fester, this is Derek and Helen.'

Fester bowed courteously to Derek. 'A new star shines at our meeting, fair Helen.'

She grabbed Helen's hand and shook it vigorously. 'Well met, Derek, me old sport!'

'I think she must be a trickster or a court jester!' said Helen. 'How exciting! I'm a bit of a free spirit myself you know!'

Fester looked at Helen with unblinking eyes. Her beak tied itself into a knot with a bow shaped like a heart. Helen clapped with delight.

The boardwalk led onto a wide platform arranged with trellises draped in white and yellow flowers. The Cluaracan and the grown-ups went ahead, crossing the platform and stepping into another walkway. We made to follow but

Fester stayed where she was and something made us stay with her. She leaned over sideways, as if peering round a corner and watched as the Cluaracan, chatting merrily, moved out of earshot.

'Now listen to me, Junior Festival Committee (Cow-Fetching Sub-group),' Fester said, and her voice sounded different, as if she was having difficulty controlling it or getting the words out. 'There's more going on here than you know. There's schemes and plots and enchantments. You are all in terrible danger. There's someone who wants to see Knockmealldown destroyed, and it's all my fault. But listen to me, listen to me; it will only get harder. If you survive the King and Queen, you must Challenge him. Challenge him for the Cloak. The Challenge of the Four Feats. For the Cloak of Feathers.'

We stared at her. She trembled and shook and flapped her wings and kicked her feet.

'Survive the King and Queen?' said Derek.

'Schemes and plots and enchantments?' said Helen.

'Challenge who?' I asked faintly, because I felt as if I was about to faint. 'Four feet?'

Fester's huge cave-eyes blinked up at me innocently.

'Come on,' called the Cluaracan. I jumped as he went striding past. I could have sworn he'd been ahead of us moments before. 'Let's not keep their majesties waiting!'

After a moment of shock and confusion we hurried to keep up with him, even though I had a distinct feeling that we should have been running the other way instead, as fast as we could.

4.

THE AUDIENCE

THE HIGH PAVILION that surrounded Long Lisa's Tower was sheltered by a sloping roof, but open on all sides to the gentle summer breezes. Gauzy drapes and curtains that fluttered, flowed and shimmered in the sunlight had been hung from the eaves. A small, tense throng of Folk stood warily inside. When I walked in, still trying to process whatever it was that Fester had tried to tell us, they stared at me with a kind of disgusted awe. I was probably the first person to try running down their Royal Family in millennia.

At the centre of the pavilion was a dais, carved out of what looked like a huge block of bog oak, with knuckled fingers rising from the back and curling protectively over the antlered heads of the King and Queen in their thrones. Much more impressive than our old pallets. Their furious Majesties were glaring poisonously across the Pond at the buildings of Ghost Pig Estate. The Cluaracan leaped dramatically forward, doffed his hat and bowed with an elaborate flourish.

'Your Majesties! It's sorry I am to interrupt your

frivolities, but I wish to present: representatives of the Knockmealldown Festival Committee!'

The King narrowed his eyes at us.

'Are they going to apologise and beg for mercy? That's what they should be doing. Never in a thousand years have I seen the like.'

'Perhaps they wish to insult us again?' said the Queen. 'Perhaps they wish to assault us and humiliate us? Before they start, someone should warn them that the protection of the Festival is an indulgence we grant, not a law we are required to obey. We are slow to respond to the grotesque horrors and personal outrages we have witnessed today only because it is a custom of long standing we are reluctant to break, and because these seem like trivialities when set against our larger concerns. But our patience is thin and it would be amusing to punish the foolish and the ill-mannered in various ways.'

'You!' the King pierced me with a stare like a pair of sharpened icicles through the eyeballs. 'What do you have to say for yourself?'

'Um, sorry?' I said. 'I'm so very sorry.'

'And are you the fellow who made such a mess of our proud and lovely lakeside? Did you dig up the land and impale it with metal and build houses and make that stench? What is it with you humans and foul smells? You have the most revolting taste in all of creation! Was that you?'

'Me? No!'

'No? A likely story!'

'Please, Your Majesties,' said Sheila. 'None of that was

59

Brian's fault – he wasn't even alive at the time!'

'That's no excuse!' barked the King. 'That's just laziness.'

'The pig factory was put in by the government!' said Bob. 'And then later the land was bought up by a developer and the houses built. We tried to stop them, but they ignored us. It had nothing to do with Brian at all!'

'We are well aware of the disgraceful destruction that has taken place here,' said the Queen. 'Believe me, we would have taken our revenge on the lot of you years ago if our own dear daughter had not spoken up in your defence at the time!'

'Our dear daughter,' said the King. 'Only her love for Knockmealldown and for the Festival protected you from our anger. Otherwise our curse would have plagued you to madness and ruination.'

'Wait,' I said. 'Your daughter stopped you from cursing Knockmealldown? But if there was no curse . . . how come we've had all the misfortune and the misery and stuff?'

The King narrowed his eyes at me.

'No curse of ours. All your misfortune is your own doing, as far as I can tell. It's quick you are to blame the Folk for troubles you made for yourselves.'

'Thank you for explaining, Your Majesties,' Sheila said. 'And where is your daughter so that we can thank her for her kind intervention on our behalf?'

'Our daughter is no longer with us,' said the Queen, and her eyes filled with tears. The King gave a sob.

'I am very sorry for your loss,' said Sheila quietly.

'Aye, we lost her,' said the King. 'She went away or was taken from us and we have not seen her since. We have searched every corner of the Otherworld. We have promised every scrap of treasure we possess, every gift, every blessing, every spell, every office, but none can find her and bring her back to us.'

'She was always the willful one,' said the Queen. 'She went her own way and did her own thing, always in her Cloak of Feathers. Perhaps she flew too high one day, out into the unreachable blue of the sky. I fear she cannot find her way home.'

'Oh!' said Helen. 'That's so sad!'

'Or maybe someone stole her Cloak of Feathers and left her stuck as half a mixed-up bird and then cast a spell that made all the Folk blind to her!' Fester piped up.

The King blinked, narrowed his eyes and peered at the place where Fester was standing. Then he cleared his throat and looked away. Fester sighed. I looked down at her.

Fester. The King and Queen couldn't see her or hear her. None of the other Folk could see her either, except for the Cluaracan who had kicked her. A missing princess. Schemes and plots and enchantments. A Cloak of Feathers. A Challenge. All of Knockmealldown destroyed. Oh Mammy, oh Daddy, she'd said. The very first words I'd heard her say.

'Are you—' I began excitedly.

'You!' barked the King. I jumped. 'We've heard enough from you! Be silent!'

'But—'

'SILENCE!' roared the King. I silenced.

'Only for our daughter's sake are we here,' said the

Queen, her voice hard as flint. 'We are in no mood for festivals and in no mood for forgiveness. There will be a Festival however, in our daughter's honour. It had better be a good one. It is up to you, the Festival Committee, to make sure that it is, or things will go badly for the people of Knockmealldown. I have a mind to make them all into birds.'

Bob stood up straight, shoulders back, chin jutting forward.

'We won't let you down,' he said. 'Will we lads?'

Mum and Dad and Sheila and Helen and Derek all nodded and agreed that they never would. I didn't move or make a sound, but out of the corner of my eye I was watching Fester, and I noticed that the Cluaracan was watching me.

Why was he watching me? For all his apparent friendliness, I realised that I didn't like him. There was a calculating glint in his eye, and behind that a kind of burning rage that was really obvious if you blocked out his enormous and friendly grin.

No. That was unreasonable. The Cluaracan was probably a perfectly nice, friendly, helpful fellow with no hand in any schemes, plots or enchantments.

'That's all sorted then!' he cried, dancing nimbly in front of the dais and bowing. 'All pleasant, amicable and amiable! No need for harsh words! Forgive and forget! Let all be happiness and frivolity! There'll be no call for punishing the rude and the clumsy as an example to others!'

The Queen raised a hand.

'I nearly forgot,' she said. 'That belligerent boy almost slipped our minds. What shall we do with him?'

The Cluaracan flickered away and I was left wilting under the full might and anger of the King and Queen of the Other Folk. My stomach tightened in sheer terror and I felt myself shake and shiver. Their eyes burned and the ivy in their hair writhed and the feathers in their dark cloaks fluttered and rippled.

'Don't you touch him!' snarled Mum, stepping in front of me.

'Let's all be reasonable about this,' said Dad, standing beside her.

The Cluaracan gasped somewhere nearby.

'The selfless nobility! They're offering themselves in his place! What a beautiful sacrifice!'

'Just a minute!' said Mum.

'There really is no need for unpleasantness,' said Dad.

'No,' said the Queen, a note of respect and appreciation in her voice. 'In light of your courage and love, we won't make this too unpleasant for you.'

'No!' I screamed. 'Don't you touch them!'

Too late. Before the first word was out of my mouth, it was done. Where Mum and Dad had been standing were two tall, thin, regal and angular herons. At the sound of my voice they slowly spread their wings and lifted off across the pavilion floor, out through the open side of the Tower, across the shining mud to a pool near the far shore where they landed and stood, each on one long, crooked, stick-like leg, and were utterly still.

'Mum?' I said. 'Dad?'

'Herons!' said the Cluaracan admiringly. 'Very nicely done, Your Majesties. They will be the guardians of this sacred place for all the long years ahead.'

'Hey now!' said Bob. 'That's just not on! You can't go around turning people into birds!'

'Yes, we can,' said the King. 'And if you're not careful we'll turn every man, woman and child in Knockmeall-down into birds, or worse! It's more birds this world needs and fewer humans!'

'Oh, they are in a very bad mood,' said Fester.

'Honour our daughter with a Festival to be remembered,' said the Queen. 'Then we might look more favourably on you.'

This had all unfolded while I stood frozen in horror, unable to move or speak. Finally the anger bubbled up inside me and burst out in a roar.

'MUM! DAD! WHAT DID YOU DO TO MY MUM AND DAD!'

'Get him out of here before he makes things worse,' I heard Sheila say. 'Quickly!'

'WORSE? I'LL GIVE YOU WORSE, YOU HAIRY HORRIBLE HORN-HEADED SHRIMPS!'

My throat was raw and I was kicking and punching, but I didn't really have anything to kick and punch at as Derek somehow lifted me up and carried me out of the pavilion and through the Floating Palace with Helen leading the way, trying to calm me down.

He dumped me on the shore of the Pond and I stopped screaming and punching and kicking and just lay there on my knees, staring out at the shimmer and shine of the

Pond. Water was flowing back into the Pond, seeping out of the mud, spreading in widening pools and streams, the mud dissolving away. Lost in the dancing sunlight were the herons standing together far away where I could never reach them. Fester flumped down beside me with a huff.

'Sorry, Brian,' she said. 'But I know how you feel.'

'I just want my mum and dad back,' I sobbed.

'Me, too,' she said. 'Me, too.'

5.

THE CHALLENGE

'WHAT AM I going to do?' I said. 'What am I going to do?'

'Well kneeling there like a great gobdaw won't help,' said Derek.

'Why did this have to happen?' I said. 'Why does everything always turn out so horrible?'

'It's Knockmealldown,' said Derek. 'Everything turns out horrible in Knockmealldown.'

'Oh, this sort of thing happens all the time in fai— uh, folk tales, Brian,' said Helen. 'They'll get changed back! Eventually. Think of the Children Of Lir! They were changed into swans and they got changed back.'

'Didn't they get changed back when they were really old and they all died?' I said.

'Oh,' said Helen. 'Yes. Oh dear.'

'Helen, this isn't one of them stories!' said Derek. 'This is real!'

'Derek, I don't know if you noticed, but folk tales *are* real, and we're in one. We have to start acting like it. Then we can get through this safely and have some fun as we go!'

'Fun?' I said. 'Helen. My mum and dad are herons.'

'Oh don't worry about them, they'll be fine! All the Folk want is a nice happy festival because that's what their Princess would have wanted! Then the King and the Queen will turn your mum and dad back to people and go away for a hundred years and that's a long time so they won't be our problem any more.'

'*Our* problem?' I said, looking up at them both. 'I mean, I'm the one they're angry with, and it's my mum and dad. You don't have to . . . y'know . . .'

'Brian,' said Helen. 'Of course we're going to help. We're the Junior Knockmealldown Festival Committee. It's our job.'

Derek shook his head.

'Hopeless,' he said. 'Flippin' hopeless, the pair of you.'

'You don't have to help!' snapped Helen. 'I know you don't like me or Brian, or anyone or anything but yourself, so you can just go away and vandalise something if that's your idea of a good time!'

Derek looked shocked.

'You think I don't like you?'

He sounded so hurt it stopped both Helen and me in our tracks. We stared at him. With a visible effort, he put a sneer back on his face.

'Well I don't! You're a snob on a horse and he's a useless mopey mammy's boy and you can both take a running bloody jump for all I care! But sure as roast chicken on a Sunday you'll mess this all up and the whole town'll get turned into worms or something and I don't want to be a worm, all right?'

That was more like it.

'Nobody wants to be a worm, Derek,' said Helen.

I suddenly felt very warm and soggy.

'Thank you, guys,' I sniffed. 'Helen's right.'

'Of course I am,' said Helen.

'Of course she is,' said Derek, rolling his eyes. 'How is she right?'

'Yes, how am I right?' said Helen.

There was a plan in my head. A weird, half-formed plan. Most of the plan didn't even exist, but there was a sort of a shape of one, like some giant object moving through space blocking out the stars.

'What we need to do . . .' I said, '. . . is run the Festival, and we run it good and we run it right. It doesn't have to be the best Festival in the world ever, either, it just has to be good enough so they don't call the whole thing off early, because that gives us today and tomorrow to sort things out.'

'What do you mean, sort things out?' said Helen.

I was up and striding back and forth along a small patch of shore, a strange feverish energy burning through me. 'I know what'll make them forgive and forget the insults and the mess that was made of the Pond and turn Mum and Dad back. We can find their daughter.'

'Their daughter?' said Helen, puzzled. Then she brightened. 'Oh, yes, a quest for this missing princess! Trapped in some terrible dungeon somewhere by an evil leprechaun! If we rescue her they'll be so grateful!'

Derek groaned.

'What are you, Law And Order Missing Pixies Unit?

Sherlock Holmes and his sidekick the Hobbit, is it? How are you even going to begin looking for a missing magical Princess, who could be anywhere, everywhere or nowhere, let alone find her in two days while keepin' a stupid Festival goin' at the same time? It's daft! It's beyond daft, it's demented!'

'Oh,' I said. 'That's the easy part. I've already found her.'

I looked over at Fester, who was standing on her head and going round and round and round like a top, her flapping beak a yellow blur.

'What?' said Derek. 'That thing? Have you completely lost the plot altogether?'

Helen, unsurprisingly, was a bit more in tune with how these things work.

'Someone put a spell on her, didn't they?' she said with a breathless gasp. 'And now nobody recognises her and they've been looking and looking for her and she's right there all along. That's diabolical! Your Majesty!'

She executed an impeccable bow, no less elegant for all the mud that still caked her riding clothes. Fester, unaware, kept flapping her arms and legs up and down on the grass.

It occurred to me that I was very lucky to have Helen on my side. I looked at Derek, who was twisting his face into a skeptical, but thoughtful scowl. I remembered some of the things I'd thought about Helen and Derek, and how I hadn't made any effort to hide them. I cringed at how I must have acted towards them. I was lucky to have anyone on my side at all, really, wasn't I?

Fester suddenly sat upright and noticed we were staring and bowing at her.

'What?' she said. 'What'd I do? I didn't do it! Leave me alone.'

'You're their missing daughter, aren't you?' I said. 'The Princess. You practically told me as much. That wasn't a trick was it? Please tell me that wasn't some sort of trick!'

She peered at me with her shadowy eyes and her beak twitched and sniffed.

'You really can hear me and speak to me, can't you?' she said, sounding amazed and delighted. 'Oh, the spell isn't as strong on humans as it is on Folk!'

She began to bounce up and down, bending her knees, flapping her wings, her beak wobbling like a long rubber tube.

'Who was it?' said Helen. 'What did he do to you? How do we fix it?'

Fester's bouncing suddenly stopped.

'My Cloak of Feathers!' she snapped. 'If I had my Cloak of Feathers again no enchantment could hold me!'

'So what are we supposed to do, then?' demanded Derek. 'Could we just, like, sew a bunch of feathers together? Would that do?'

Fester made no answer, but suddenly went stiff as a board and toppled over backwards. We stared at her. I was about to start yelling at her in frustration when the Cluaracan fell out of the sky.

He landed with a jaunty skip, and everything about him seemed to suggest lively good cheer and friendliness.

But I knew better. In fact, I knew more than that; I knew what he'd done. He'd deliberately reminded the King and Queen about me, and then when Mum and Dad had tried to protect me he'd provoked the King and Queen into transforming them.

And as far as I could tell, he was the only one of the Folk who could see Fester.

'Greetings, oh Junior Committee Members!' He smiled, and all I could see was a row of crooked yellow teeth. His brown tweed coat billowed as he bowed, and I could see its lining was dark and smooth and shiny.

Since the birds had started to fly that morning, part of me had been floating, as if I were in bed, half-dreaming, watching shadows dance on my ceiling. The astonishing host of Folk, saying the *f* word, rolling down on the King and Queen, Fester's strange outbursts, the audience on the pavilion, the horror of what had happened to Mum and Dad; I felt them all, but as if from a distance, as if I knew I couldn't take the full brunt of all that confusion and amazement and grief.

Now, though. Now I came back. Now I felt it all whirling and mixing inside me, like the crazy ingredients of Sheila's bread, until what was left was cold, round, hard, and dangerous. I knew.

What had Fester said? *There's schemes and plots and enchantments . . . He wants to see Knockmealldown destroyed.*

'I Challenge you,' I said to the Cluaracan. He blinked at me. What words had Fester used? It was important to get it right. 'The Challenge of the Four Feats. For the Cloak of Feathers. I Challenge you.'

If I had managed to shock the Cluaracan, he hid it well. His smile didn't budge by so much as a millimetre. His eyes told a different story, but not one that I could read.

'Are you saying he has the Cloak?' said Helen, wonderingly.

'Oi, you!' barked Derek. 'Give up that oul' Cloak before we turn you into horse-feed!'

The Cluaracan ignored us, turning his gaze to Fester, who was spinning around on her head again.

'Stop that,' he told her. She fell on her face. 'What have you been telling these impressionable children, you wretch? More of your lies? Brian, don't listen to her. Withdraw this Challenge before you get hurt. Before you lose. Did she tell you what would happen to you if you lose even one part of the Challenge?'

My mouth felt dry and I had difficulty swallowing. I shook my head.

'We take you away with us,' said the Cluaracan gently. 'You live forever as our servant in the Otherworld. Unlike those we bring as guests and friends, you will waste away, becoming grey and faint and transparent, a lost soul in a torment of limbo. Withdraw your Challenge or you will never see your parents again, never feel rain or sunlight on your face. Never hear the rustling of green things or the singing of the birds.'

A cold sweat broke out all over me, and all the strength went from my legs. Why was I doing this? I hated Knockmealldown. I barely knew this feathery scrap of a Folk person. The Cluaracan seemed so friendly and reasonable.

72

But Mum and Dad were herons because of him. And Fester looked on the outside like the lonely mess of a freak I felt on the inside. Making things right was never easy, and if I didn't do it, who would?

'I Challenge you,' I whispered before I could stop myself.

The Cluaracan was no longer smiling. His face was serious, and there was contempt in the way he looked at me.

'Very well then,' he said. 'Let it be so. This wretched Festival may end up being more entertaining than I was anticipating. Don't think you'll save her, though, or your moon-eyed parents, or this vile village. You won't even save yourselves. Those that don't end up as birds will moan forever as wraiths in the haunted places of the Otherworld.'

'Okay,' I said, a drum beating in my head. 'I guess she's not a liar then.'

'You'll wish she was, and that she'd never uttered a word of truth before this is over, me bucko. I will divide the Cloak in four, and if you manage to perform a Feat to my satisfaction, you will be told where to find a piece.'

'What,' I said, through a mouth full of cotton wool. 'What are the Feats?'

I don't know what I was imagining. I really hadn't thought this through. What if he asked me for the golden apples of the sun or the tooth of a dragon or Darth Vader's helmet? Oh God, I was doomed.

'Those?' he said, suddenly smiling and twinkling again. 'Why, that is up to me. Let's start with one of your very own devising!' He waved a crumpled copy of the Official Festival Timetable at me. 'The Family Fun and Historical Cycle! Succeed and you will become the proud owner of the first piece of Cloak. And then I will advise you of your next Challenge.'

I stared at the evil, grinning rogue. Was this some sort of trick? A Cycle? How could a Cycle be a Feat? Either it was a trick, or the Good Folk vastly overestimated the accomplishment of riding a bicycle. Still, at least I wouldn't have to cycle to the sun or anything.

'I'm sorry, but I'm finding this confusing,' said Helen, who didn't look confused at all. 'What is the Feat supposed to be? We need to decide before the Cycle exactly what it is Brian has to do.'

'A legal mind, I see,' said the Cluaracan, clapping his hands together and rubbing them vigorously. 'Quite right. Set the terms now to avoid disagreements later, eh? Seeing as it's the Festival and all, I'm amenable to keeping the first Feat simple and straightforward. We won't be asking you to recover a single string from the Golden Harp hidden in an egg in the belly of an eagle perched on the summit of the highest mountain in the world!'

He studied me again and gave a little wince of pity, unimpressed. He held up the programme, tracing a stubby finger along the crude little map that showed a dotted line running from the Green to Main Street, up to the church, then out in a loop, through Cullen's Cross, back along the lower road, through the Estate and down to the Green again.

'I think we'll all be hugely impressed if you manage to

guide this Family Fun and Historical Cycle along its route and bring it back safely within the allotted time of – what does it say here? Three quarters of an hour? That sets the bar at the right height, don't you agree?'

'Really?' I said.

'That's a doddle!' said Derek. 'Can you not make it interesting?'

'Shut up!' hissed Helen.

'Really,' said the Cluaracan.

He was lying. I felt sick with certainty. He was lying, and this was a trick, but what could I do? I was in it, now. Stick to the plan, I told myself. Such as it was. Get the Cloak. Free Fester. Save my parents and Knockmealldown. No problem.

'Right,' I said. 'I'll lead it, then. Everyone who wants to go will gather at the Green in an hour. *If* anyone wants to go, that is.'

'Oh, I hope they do,' said the Cluaracan. 'Or you'll lose by default. See you in one of your human hours, then!'

He twirled his blackthorn stick and sauntered away in the direction of the Floating Palace.

'I hope you fall in,' Helen told his retreating back.

'And get eaten by a pike,' said Derek.

The Cluaracan walked lightly, but I felt so heavy I thought I was going to break the surface of the earth and fall down through the ground and out the other side of the world and into outer space, dragged to the bottom of the universe by the weight of it all, the responsibility and the fear and the confusion.

'I'll go get my bike then,' I said, and left the Green and

the Floating Palace and the Good Folk and my parents the birds and went back to Ghost Pig Estate. Though Helen and Derek and Fester came with me, I felt as if I was walking alone.

6.

ABOUT A BICYCLE

WE WERE STANDING outside my house, on the hard clay that was supposed to be our front lawn. On the road behind us people were going past in dribs and drabs. We had to pause every few minutes to yell and wave at them to go around the deadly covered pot hole. Bob and Sheila were frantically running between the village and the Green, rousting people out and sending them down with their bicycles. They just thought they were trying to make sure everyone didn't get turned into birds. They didn't even know about the Challenge.

Derek was holding my Backahatchi. He bent over, examining it in detail, muttering to himself and shaking his head as if every dent, scratch and crack hadn't been put there by him. Once it had been my pride and joy. A Backahatchi sixteen-gear multi-lever hybrid mountain-racer with a gravity-fed rotating brake system and gyroscopic shock absorbers to cancel out every bump in the road. It had gleamed and whirred as I rode it up mountains and through woods and across bogs, along miles and miles and miles of roads. I had been looking forward to exploring every track and boreen and animal trail for a fifty-mile radius around Knockmealldown on my beloved Backahatchi.

'Has anyone ever told you that this place smells like the third day after a battle in a dungheap?' said Fester. 'Because if they did they're wrong. It's worse than that.'

'It's banjaxed,' Derek declared. 'Not even worth stealing.'

'You'd know,' I said through grinding teeth. 'You're the one who stole it and banjaxed it.'

'Hey, I haven't touched it in ages!' said Derek. 'I've done my time and paid for my crimes. I'm all reformed now. Forgive and forget, like. Anyway, you won't get far on this. Will I get you another one?'

'No!'

'Then you're stuck with it and good luck to you. Now do you think we could stop messing' about with your stupid bicycle and ask the talkin' mophead over there what the heck is goin' on? Is she really this missin' princess and can she save us all from bein' turned into centipedes?'

'Maybe we could talk about it somewhere else?' Helen peered about uneasily.

'This cursed spot is shunned by human and Folk alike,' said Fester as a family of about twelve, from tiny children to sprightly grandparents, went by, waving hello and trying not to breathe too deeply.

'Go round that bit!' we yelled, pointing at the pot hole. 'Go round!'

'Yes, go round the pit of doom!' yelled Fester. 'So we can chatter away privately to our heart's content until the Hëlweed climbs our legs, wraps itself round our throats and fills our mouths with poisonous red flowers!'

Helen squeaked. Derek gagged. Fester looked at them in surprise.

'You do know Hëlweed is a plant from the Otherworld, don't you? It's not supposed to be here at all. Mighty warriors, dragons and giant eagles alike live in fear of the horrible Hëlweed. Another gift from the Cluaracan, I suppose.'

'Cheerful one, aren't you?' said Derek.

'You'd be of a sunny disposition too if some warty mouth-breathing gombeen of a *maistín* had stolen your Cloak of Feathers and left you caught in an unnatural state of jumbled-up bird and Folk! If they hadn't cast a mean, cruel and dirty glamour so all your friends and everyone you knew barely saw you or heard you! So you spent every day and every night with your own grieving parents right before your very eyes, and they tearing themselves apart with terror, loss and rage while you try to tell them that you're right there in front of them! And that villain! Consoling them and advising them and smirking behind his hands the whole time! Oh you'd be cheerful too!'

She had slumped down to the ground, her thick yellow legs splayed, her wings hanging uselessly by her sides, her beak drooping and her eyes like high windows into long lonely nights lying awake staring at nothing, filled with pain and despair.

I sat down beside her and took in some deep breaths.

'How could he be so cruel?' I said, disbelieving. 'That's horrible, Fester. I'm so sorry.'

'Oh you poor thing,' said Helen, kneeling down and resting one hand on Fester's shoulder. Derek clenched and unclenched his fists.

'In front of your mam and dad?' he said. 'Right there in front of them? That's rotten. That's foul. That's unspeakable, that is. We'll do it. We'll get you back your Cloak. We'll fix it. We'll get you back to your mam and your dad.'

'We will,' said Helen.

I stared at the two of them, regretting every bad thing I'd ever thought about them.

'Yeah,' I said. 'We'll try, anyway. So what happened? How'd you get into this mess? Can you tell us? A short version though, we've only half an hour left.'

Just then a terrible squeal tore across the empty houses, the coiling Hëlweed and the desolation of the road. We jumped in shock and terror, and then froze.

'Run!' cried Helen, but none of us could move.

Hooves thumped on the brown clay of the road. The huge bulk of the giant boar came trotting nimbly towards us. The tiny agile legs and the enormous body just didn't seem to fit together in my mind and yet there it was, powering straight at us, red eyes glowing, tusks dripping with condensation.

Fester stood up and held out her wings.

'Oh, ivy and oak and all things green! Mulkytine! Mulkytine my old friend, do you know me at all? Surely you, most cunning and bloody-minded of them all, can see through his rotten illusions!'

'Fester!' I hissed. 'Fester get behind us!'

Instead she staggered forward.

'No, look, he knows me! He knows me!'

All three of us reached for her. Mulkytine accelerated, and with a speed that would have been sickening if I'd had long enough to feel sick, he crossed the road, his head lowered so that it was between his forelegs, his snout almost scraping the ground. The tusks were yellow and dirty and jagged, as ancient as stone axes dug out of the hillsides.

'It's me,' said Fester. 'She who would not hunt.'

Four trotters dug into the red clay, scraping deep furrows, spitting clods and pebbles in every direction. A huge bellowing breath gushed out of Mulkytine's snout. His raging eyes seemed to swallow Fester down. I spat clay and pebbles from my mouth, my face stinging from the flying stones. Fester stretched out a wing and rubbed his shaggy, spiny head.

'You great big side o' bacon, you,' said Fester, choking slightly. 'How've you been?'

Mulkytine shook and shuddered, and she scratched behind a torn and ragged ear. Fester looked up at us with her huge dark eyes and her strange yellow beak.

'Listen to me and I'll tell you everything,' she said.

7.

FESTER'S FEATHERS

'**I WAS NOT** always the ridiculous creature you see before you,' Fester began. 'Once I was pretty, and tall, for my kind. I wore my Cloak of Feathers, a gift of friendship from the Queen of the Birds herself. Ah, many were the adventures the Queen and I had together. We saved the Kingdom of the Bears from a lost volcano that drifted into the icy lands and threatened to melt all the snow. We rescued children from underground Grogglers. We snatched tiny chicks from the hands of wicked children. With my Cloak of Feathers I could become any bird I wished, though I favoured the mischievous magpie, the rogue of silver and black, the sneaky thief, the braggart and bully! Often would I fly through the clouds on the breast of the cold north wind and feel worlds appear and disappear below me!

'But the Cluaracan, the cruel and wicked and cunning Cluaracan! Once a beggar and mendicant tailor, he took residence in the cellars of Landlords and Earls and drank their wine and brandy and played childish tricks for his own amusement. He listened to their talk and aped their ways, and he longed to embrace it, and conceived an aristocratic ambition of his own. He decided to fall in love with a princess! Oh, his love is real, and all the more revolting for it. A contrived love can be undermined and shown to be false, but he fell in love completely and so it cannot be gainsayed.

'"Marry me!" he begged before the assembled multitudes of human and Folk at the last Great Festival. On one knee he knelt, one hand on his heart and the other proffering a ring with a diamond tunnelled from the heart of a mountain, cut with the teeth of an iron dwarf and polished with dragon-hide. His smile, so charming and sincere, his eyes brimming with adoration. But I do not want to be adored. I told him no. I did not laugh, whatever he may say. I was gentle and kind as I could be, for I did not know then the extent of his malignancy. The crowd did not mock; they ached with sympathy at his rejection. But his humiliation was absolute. In his rage he blamed me, even as he loved me still.

'But I didn't care. My life went on as before, full of adventures and songs and freedom and friends. Until . . . until . . .'

Fester was stammering and stumbling over her words. It was the first time I'd seen her look confused and uncertain. I heard a rustling and a creaking noise, and something came slithering across the road. I whirled round, and saw a long tendril of Hëlweed lying in the dirt; perfectly still, perfectly innocent, just peacefully photosynthesising in the sunlight. Except it hadn't been there a moment before, and like a long, thin finger, it was pointing right at us. Mulkytine, moving slowly and silently, placed himself between us and the Hëlweed. Helen and Derek nervously shuffled to keep Fester between them and Mulkytine.

'Is it supposed to do that?' said Derek in a faint voice.

'This may be the wrong place to tell *that* story after all,' said Fester, taking a step back from the Hëlweed. 'I'll skip to the end. There was a chase. I flew as a magpie and he rode a gale of wind, clutching at my tail-feathers. Down through the entrance to the Otherworld I landed, transforming, but I was only halfway back to my own true shape when his strong hands wrenched the Cloak from my back, and I was left, dazed and confused, trapped in the grotesque form you see before you, my own powers checked.'

I listened to her speak, but my eyes were fixed on the Hëlweed. I was sure I could see it twitch and wriggle like a worm, inching nearer. Mulkytine snorted and made a little dash forward, his hooves kicking up a little cloud of dust. The Hëlweed twitched back.

'Once he had my Cloak, I was in his power. He wove a subtle charm around me. None could recognise me in my current form. I was a half-thing that could only be half-seen, half-heard by other Folk, as if from the corner of the eye or the tip of the ear. When the alarm was raised and the search began I was there waving my wings, screaming my name until I was hoarse with weeping. I had to watch my own mother and father sink into bitterness and despair, watch the grinning maggot responsible comfort and advise them. So I beg you. Forgive the King and Queen. They are not themselves. They are out of their minds with loss and they are being cruelly manipulated.'

She took a deep breath, as if exhausted.

'Janey mack, I haven't spoken so long to anyone for a dog's age! And have them listen, too! You've been a great audience altogether, so you have; be sure to tip the waiting staff.'

Mulkytine stood before Fester and bowed his head, then turned and trotted away. I heard the distant clatter of a hundred hooves and a small herd of transparent pink pig bodies seemed to follow after him as he ran across the crooked finger of Hëlweed, crushing it and tearing it apart, but when I blinked they were gone.

Fester's shoulders were slumped and her wings hung limp and her beak drooped. I tilted my head at the others, and we turned away and quietly and without any fuss set to work making the bike roadworthy again.

It was fiddly and awkward. The poor thing would have completely fallen apart under the slightest strain; but Derek's strong, clever fingers tightened here, bent there, pushed this and pulled that until the front wheel was almost back where it was supposed to be and not likely to fall out unless it ran into something rough and destructive, like a stiff breeze or a piece of straw on the road. Derek seemed to know as much about fixing bikes as he did about breaking them. When we'd done as much as we could, I set it upright and we headed for the Green.

'Are you coming, Fester?' said Helen. The odd, ageless, shapeless little Folk girl was still staring off into the spaces between empty houses and Hëlweed.

'You don't want to miss Brian falling off his bike,' said Derek. 'It never stops being funny.'

She whirled round and ran up to join us, her feathers shaking, her beak wobbling.

'Go on, Brian,' she said. 'Tom Tinny O'Flourihan would be proud.'

'Who the heck is Tom Tinny O'Flourihan?' I asked. I think they were trying to distract me from what was coming next. It wasn't really working, but it was nice of them to try.

'Did you never hear about the great race between Tom Tinny on his bike and Mike Costigan on his horse? Listen to me now and I'll tell you . . .'

I lost track of what she was saying. All I could hear was the slight crunch of the wheels of my bicycle on the ground. It's simple, I told myself. Just a quick, easy, pleasant cycle.

But this was the Knockmealldown Summer Festival, where nothing was ever simple.

8.
THE CYCLE

BOB AND SHEILA had been busy. Seasoned organisers, they'd rounded up confused and frightened Knockmealldowners and their bikes and sent them all down to the Green, waiting for their leader and guide. The cyclists weren't happy. The Good Folk were not being particularly friendly or festive and there were disquieting rumours to do with threats and dark promises and people being turned into things. A few had hopped in their cars and tried to leave, but after they'd gone a mile they found themselves turned round and driving back in again. Now they were expected to take part in this farce, cycling around like a bunch of eejits behind a slip of a lad who wasn't even a local, but a blow-in, *a blow-in*, mind.

Bob and Sheila tried to calm them down and explain the situation: Mum and Dad were now herons, off fishing for frogs and mice at the far side of the lake, and if we didn't want to join them we'd better go along with this farce and smile like pop-eyed presenters on a kid's TV show while doing it or so help me I'll do for you. (That was Bob, who can be big and looming and threatening when he wants to be.)

There was, at least, some sympathy for me – the boy whose parents were now herons – but people were keeping slightly away from me in case my bad luck was contagious.

There were old men and women on ancient boneshakers, there were small children on tiny pink and blue bikes with training wheels, there were battered racers and mountain bikes and there were one or two sleek, gleaming, well-oiled machines that made my mouth water, ridden by sleek athletic people in sleek athletic clothing, streamlined helmets and vaguely alien-looking sunglasses. Tom Tracey and Tricia Mulligan were there, ignoring each other, sneering at me, surrounded by friends and supporters.

'So what's going to happen?' said Derek. 'What's he going to do? He must be plannin' on doin' something.'

'Oh dear,' said Helen. 'I'm not sure about this. Should you be taking all these people out with you? Things might get really . . . strange. People might get hurt or scared.'

'They're already scared,' said Derek. 'And they're in this too with the rest of us.'

'They don't know the details about the Challenge, though,' I fretted guiltily. 'No one does, except us. I don't know. Maybe Helen's right. Maybe we should call it off?'

'Yes, but then we'll all get turned into birds except you, and you'll be turned into a horrible phantom,' said Helen glumly. 'You can't let the Cycle be a walkover for the Cluaracan.'

'Caught between the Folk and a bike race,' said Fester sympathetically. 'I think the others won't be in too much danger, Brian, if that makes you feel better. Hurting people at the Great Festival isn't generally allowed. Of course, you're doing a Challenge, so you're different. You'll be in the most awful deadly peril.'

'That does make me feel better,' I muttered, and pushed the bike out onto the road. Sheila gave me a yellow vest and a pack with a first aid kit and a two-way radio that didn't actually work.

The Good Folk arrived, streaming off the Floating Palace, milling around, watching with great interest. You wouldn't have called them jolly, exactly, but they seemed to have relaxed a little. They regarded bicycles as amazing, wondrous machines. Two small elegant thrones and an exquisitely woven awning were set up on the platform. The King and Queen seated themselves, their faces cool and distant.

The auld fella was standing next to Lackley the cow, playing a lively little tune that made the blood rush a little faster and the breath go a little deeper. Everyone felt a trickle of life and energy light up their feet and their fingertips, and they held their handlebars and rested their feet on their pedals, ready to be off.

I found myself wishing Derek and Helen were coming along too, but Helen didn't have a bike and Derek was legally forbidden from riding another one until he was twenty-five. They grinned and gave me the thumbs-ups, or at least Helen did. Derek stuck his tongue out, made a grotesque face, ran his finger along his throat, then grinned and pointed at me. I scowled back at him, and cleared my throat. Time to get this over with.

'Okay!' I called, trying to sound as if I knew what I was doing. 'Follow me!'

I pushed off, and the crowd on their bikes pushed off after me. I did a big curve round onto the Green, passing in front of the platform. Good Folk parted to let me through, and the Cycle followed, wobbly and awkward, as a crowd of cyclists all trying to do a slow one-hundred-and-eighty degree turn at the same time tends to be. As I passed the platform, I saw the King and Queen, faces impassive, and sat straighter on my saddle. The Cluaracan, standing beside the platform, had doffed his hat and was waving it at us in circles.

Two herons were standing on the water, close to the shore. My foot slipped off the pedal, and the crossbar nearly cut me in half. I struggled and veered and wobbled until I was upright again.

Impressive, Brian, I thought.

Through the Estate we went, suspensions rattling on the atrocious road like a box of children's toys rolling down a mountainside. I hoped the road wouldn't destroy the bikes and that Mulkytine wouldn't turn up and destroy the people. We made it through, shaken but intact.

I led the Cycle onto Main Street, and up the winding hill that led to the T-junction in front of the church. I was in the middle of the road, and the Cycle followed behind in two streams. At the head of one, on my left, was Tricia. At the head of the other was Tom. A few of the Good Folk had made it through the Estate with us and were following along on the footpaths, but now they were gradually dropping behind.

Mentally, I charted the course that would take us on a loop out of Knockmealldown to Cullen's Cross and then down the lower road, back to the Pond and the Green. It was a short, gentle route, because you can't expect little kids on little bikes to go very far or very fast. The whole point was for a relaxed excursion to take in some of the scenery and sights and points of historical interest. What the Good Folk were getting out of it I had no idea. They'd all lost interest and wandered off long before we reached the church.

'You'll be goin' left here, won't you Brian?' Tricia said.

'Hang a right here, Brian,' said Tom. 'That's the best way.'

'Nobody but an eejit would go right,' Tricia said. 'That's a bad road, all rocky and rough.'

'You don't want to be goin' left at all,' said Tom. 'You can't see a thing that way, it's all blocked this time of the year.'

'Left is gorgeous, Brian,' said Tricia. 'Smooth and scenic and easy as a fireman slidin' down a pole.'

'Right is packed with stuff to see,' said Tom. 'You could spend a year tellin' stories about the stuff down on the right, Brian.'

'Suit yourself, though,' said Tricia, testily.

'Ah, go wherever ye like, then,' said Tom, waspishly.

I wobbled. I veered. The Cycle wobbled and veered behind me. The route on the map was just a dotted line. I didn't have to follow it. We could go either way. Both routes were short loops that would bring us back to the Green. I was free to choose my own adventure! The entire universe could hinge on this choice! Left-right, left-right!

Suddenly it was like trying to choose death by hanging or firing squad.

I shut my eyes, and breathed, and went right, the way I'd always planned to go. Tom radiated smug approval and Tricia glowered angry resentment, and neither of them spoke to me for the rest of the Cycle.

9.
THE LAST RIDE OF THE BACKAHATCHI
3000

THE ROAD RAN gently downhill through fields and farms and hedges. The sun was shining, and a light breeze made the leaves on the trees dance, so that their shadows rippled like cool dark pools as we passed over them. The two lines of Traceys and Mulligans had mingled together, and Tricia and Tom had drifted towards the back, like unappreciated guardian angels in a sulk.

I stopped the Cycle at Cullen's Cross for a rest and to let stragglers catch up before starting the last leg back to the Pond, desperately concealing my growing sense of urgency. Everybody was having a nice time, chatting and smiling. I couldn't take credit for it, but at least nothing had gone wrong. It was probably the first time in decades that a Festival event had gone so well, so pleasantly, so enjoyably, for up to – I checked my watch again – twenty whole minutes! A new record! That left twenty-five minutes to get back, and it was downhill most of the way. Plenty of time, but close enough to make me incredibly nervous and anxious. I smiled and laughed, while inside I was wound up, tense and scared. I knew it couldn't be this easy. I knew something bad was coming.

'Come on, guys!' I called, with forced jollity. 'Time to get moving again!'

That was the moment when we all felt something shiver its way up our spines. We lifted our heads like antelope at a watering hole catching the faint scent of hungry predator on the breeze. The friendly chatter stopped. Heads turned. Mums and dads moved protectively towards their children.

The screaming started somewhere far off, like the unpleasant buzzing of a terrifying carnivorous insect that fills you with a deep and primitive fear, blooming at the base of your spine and flowing down to your toes and up to the top of your head. Bells chimed as the hands holding the bikes shivered and shook. No cloud moved in the sky, yet the sun seemed to dim and the air grew chill.

The screaming came across the sky. Over the fields. Along the roads. Voices raised in long, high, terrible wails of grief.

'Lord protect us,' Tricia said. 'It's the banshee.'

'It's a lot of banshees,' said a small child, and burst out crying. Everyone looked at me.

'Do something!' someone said to me.

The screaming came round a far-off bend, down the fourth road off Cullen's Cross, the one that led away from Knockmealldown. The screaming was riding bicycles. We all stared. We saw long, dirty fingers gripping handlebars, bony elbows high, bonier knees pumping, filthy bare feet on pedals, backs hunched, heads down low, and long,

long streams of billowing hair. There were four of them on bikes coming straight at us like competitors in the Tour de Hell.

'We're going to die!' said the child.

'Aye,' said Mrs Keane, a sweet little old woman wearing a floral sun-hat. 'It comes for us all. But not today.'

With a screech of rubber, she was away down the road, legs moving like pistons on a steam train. Her floral sun hat flew off her head and landed in the ditch.

Banshees. They were the most dreaded and feared of the Good Folk. Their crying and wailing was only heard when death was coming for someone, and, once heard, nothing could stop it.

The Family Fun Cycle started to move in a panic, bumping, cutting across each other, pushing and yelling. Tricia and Tom tried to keep everyone from getting tangled. A child fell. It was all falling apart. I wanted to follow Mrs Keane and pass her and leave everybody behind to keep the banshees busy while I cycled to Australia.

Mum and Dad wouldn't like that. Even heron-Mum and heron-Dad would have disapproved. I was in charge. I had to do something. Otherwise my mum and dad would be birds forever, and so would everyone else, and the flippin' Cluaracan would laugh himself sick and probably blow his nose on Fester's Cloak of Feathers for all I knew.

I had to get the Cycle back to the Green. I had to do something about the banshees.

'Hold it!' I yelled at the panicking Cycle. 'Wait! Stop!'

They didn't stop, but they slowed down a bit in their scramble and stared at me with hopeless terror. I pointed.

'Go! Head back to the Green!' I said, waving one person down the road back to the village. 'Now you! No, you! You stop! Wait! Let him go first, and her. All the way back to the Green, everybody! It'll be safe there! Now go on, move out, go on, on you go, now you, now go on, all of you, go, go, go!'

They all moved off in more or less good order at different speeds, spreading out in a long line. They'd never outrun the banshees. One of the children stopped to pick up the fallen sun-hat while her parents broke down into hysterics.

'What about you?' Tom said. I put a foot on the pedal, fixed the strap of my helmet under my chin, gripped my handlebars and stared down at the banshees, nearly on top of us.

'Don't mind me,' I said. 'Go!'

They went. They went slowly, the last few stragglers wobbling on their tiny little bikes as their parents desperately tried to hurry them up, and the banshees, their piercing wails of raw grief filling my ears and my head, bore down on us. I could see blood-shot eyes through strands of hair and glimpse their crooked mouths, slightly open, as if groaning in pain.

'AAAAAH!' screamed the banshees.

The Cycle was as far as it was going to get before the banshees arrived. I turned straight for them, stood on my pedal, pushed down, clicking to highest gear, my legs churning, the wheels turning.

'AAAAAAAAH!' I screamed.

'AAAAAAAAH!' They screamed back at me.

'AAAAAAAAAAAAAAAAAH!'

'AAAAAAAAH!'

'AAAAAAAAAAAH ohgodohgodohgod . . .'

'AAAAAAAAH!'

I was screaming, they were screaming, the Cycle were screaming, all one big scream. I swerved sharply in front of the oncoming banshees, leaning right over, one foot out on the ground, wheels skidding, gravel flying, then up again, climbing gears, and the banshees turned to follow right behind me, almost beside me. They followed me, and I was leading them back the way we'd come, away from the Cycle. We were spread out across the road like an arrow, me at the tip, face frozen with effort and terror, and beside me and around me the bloodcurdling wail.

'WHEEEEEEEEEEEEEEEEE!'

Wait. These didn't sound like the bone-freezing screams of terrifying harbingers of mortal doom . . .

This wasn't a chase. They weren't chasing me. They were *following* me.

They hadn't been sweeping down on the Family Fun and Historical Cycle to doom us with death. They had been *joining* the Family Fun and Historical Cycle.

The road swept by under my wheels. The hedges and trees jerked like sped-up film. I wondered if I should try to say something.

'Over there you can see the ruined cottage where . . .'

No. Gone.

We swept round bends.

'HAHAHAHAHAHAHAHAHAWHOOOOOOOOO!'

Now I wasn't just scared. I was scared and embarrassed. What had taken the Cycle twenty minutes to cover, we were shooting over in no time flat. I saw the church ahead, the gable of the priest's house poking out from behind the steeple, and the T-junction at the top of Main Street. I wondered if I should make a hand signal for the turn. What the heck. Safety first. I made the signal.

They moved closer around me. Their hair, rippling in the wind, whipped at my face, tickling my cheeks, my nose, making me sneeze, getting in my mouth, my ears, covering my eyes. Blinded, clawing the hair from my eyes with one hand, I began to wobble and swerve across the road. The banshees wobbled and swerved with me. I turned the handlebar jerkily, trying to nudge us down onto Main Street, and the handlebar came off in my hand.

'AAAAAAAAAAAAAAH!'

I kept pedalling, gripping the loose handlebars as if they were welded to my fingers. I can cycle with no hands. No problem! But at high speed? Turning onto Main Street? Surrounded by banshees? Complicated! I tried to slot the handlebars back into the shaft, but I kept missing and nearly overbalancing. The brake cables were still attached, so I couldn't just drop it.

Past Bellamore's Stores, the banshees' hair billowing over me so I seemed to be sweeping down a tunnel of black and grey and silver strands. I leaned left and right to follow the swerve of the road.

Past the pubs, and my foot slipped and a pedal flew off and clattered on the road. I lurched to follow, but strands of hair pulled me back and held me upright. I had one foot stuck straight out and the other going up and down and the loose handlebars still in my hands. The other pedal went. The chain fell off and slithered along the road beneath me like a racing snake. My two legs were stuck straight out and only the banshees' hair was keeping me on the saddle, but the bike was not slowing or falling and the 'WHEEEE' of the banshees was turning into giggles.

We shot past the post office, headed for the Estate and the Green and the Pond. My front wheel separated from the bike and was rolling alongside me. My back wheel was rolling along on the other side. Their hair was the only thing holding me up. The banshees were not slowing and neither was I. When we shot into Ghost Pig Estate, my wheelless, handlebarless, pedalless bike was flying inches over the ground.

The banshees were going so fast over the rutted road they began to vibrate until they were blurring around the edges. The houses went past, and the Hëlweed.

Oh no. The Hëlweed.

Our house came round the bend and the carpet of weed over the hole in the road.

'Looook ooooooooouuuuuttttt!' I cried through chattering teeth. They didn't hear or they didn't understand or didn't care, and we swept across the hole without plunging into its gaping maw. The Hëlweed seemed to leap and writhe, clutching at us as we crossed the hole. Whirring spokes chopped the weed to scraps and shreds that flew in a cloud of petals and sap.

We flew out of the Estate and mounted the Green. People and Good Folk scattered left and right. The King and Queen were on the podium. The banshees wheeled towards the Pond. Their hair unravelled around me and I was suddenly dropped. The front fork of my bike sank into the earth. The back of the bike flew up and I was thrown forward, upside down, straight at the podium.

Something soft hit me, or I hit something soft, a feathery cushion that caught me and dragged me down and softened the blow when I landed on the ground. I rolled and the cushion rolled and I squawked and the cushion squawked. I glimpsed yellow bird-feet and a long thin yellow stalk. We rolled apart and came to a stop on the grass in front of the podium.

For a mad split second I wanted to hop up, strike a pose and say 'Ta-dah!' Then the pain and the dizziness caught up with me and I just wanted to throw up and cry.

'Urgh,' I said. 'Argh.'

Fester jumped up, struck a pose and said: 'Ta-dah!' Then she fell over again.

Hands helped me up, steadied me. One hand was patting me on the back, another gripped my shoulder firmly.

'Are you all right?' said Helen. 'That was amazing!'

'Never in all my born days!' said Derek. 'Nothing broken?'

'No,' I said. 'Nothing broken.'

'Except the bike,' said Helen.

'My bike!' I moaned.

'Blaze of glory,' said Derek. 'It's what it would have wanted. Torn apart by banshees.'

'Lucky it was just the bike,' said Helen. 'There. Can you stand?'

'Yeah,' I said, still wobbling. 'Thanks guys. Oh God it was a disaster. It was a mess. There were banshees. They had bicycles. They scared the bejaykers out of everyone and there was nearly a riot. I'm sorry lads, I think I made an awful mess of it. Uh, did anyone see where the banshees got to?'

'Oh, not far,' said Helen, pointing.

The banshees were screaming up and down the walkways and platforms of the Floating Palace. Their wheels thumped on the wooden boards as they leaped over the hump-backed bridges and did wheelies through the awnings and hops on the tables. They screamed and wailed, going 'Whooooooooooooo!' and 'Wheeeeeeeeeeeeee!'

'Whose bright idea was it to give *them* bikes?' I heard Bob wonder. He and Sheila were standing with the crowd that had slowly gathered back on the Green after fleeing for their lives. Nobody seemed sure as to whether this was hilarious or a disaster. Or a hilarious disaster.

'That was foolish,' said the King. He and the Queen had watched it all happen without moving, without expression.

At the edge of the platform the Cluaracan was leaning on his blackthorn stick with one leg crossed in front of the other. He wasn't smiling now. He was studying me thoughtfully. I bowed my head and looked at the ground. So much for Challenges and Feats. So much for getting Fester's Cloak and rescuing Mum and Dad and saving the Knockmealldowners. So much for me.

'Look at them,' said the King. 'They're supposed to be ragged avatars haunting humanity with the curse of their own mortality, not a troupe of two-wheeled acrobats.'

A banshee went over a bridge standing on the saddle of her bike with both hands outstretched.

'It's undignified,' said the King.

'Worse than that,' said the Queen. 'The Festival has been disrupted by this act of terror. Brian Nolan, we should hold you responsible for this.'

'Um,' I said, sick and dizzy. The ground had nearly stopped moving in waves, but now my body felt like it was going to collapse in on itself.

'It seems to us that this was an unfortunate misjudgement, Brian Nolan,' said the King. Something very odd was happening to his face as he said it, as if he was about to undergo another magical transformation. 'You had no business taking such bold and dangerous actions.'

The King and the Queen glared down at me. The Good Folk and the humans crowded round the edge of the Green, looking worried and serious.

Then the Queen laughed.

'But in fairness – it was hilarious!'

The King roared. 'By the hokey, the looks on their faces!'

'Banshees on bicycles!' gasped the Queen.

'Did you ever see the like?'

'Not in all my born days!'

'Oh she would have loved it, wouldn't she?'

'She would have laughed for a month!'

They went still, but fond smiles lingered on their lips and they looked into each other's eyes, as if suddenly filled with warm memories. There was still pain, though. So much pain.

The hilarity spread. People and Folk began to smile and giggle and slap each other on the back and tell each other what a great big bunch of eejits they'd been. The Good Folk slapped their thighs – if they had thighs – and held their sides and soon the Green was one mass of laughing, rolling, crying, aching hilarity.

Except me. I was so relieved I nearly cried. But I still wasn't sure. Had I won this part of the Challenge? Had I done a Feat? Had everyone in the Cycle safely made it back to the Green? Had they been in time?

Helen gave me a nudge and hissed in my ear. 'He's coming!'

The Cluaracan strolled up, swinging his stick and kicking his heels and studying the sky like a farmer casually assessing the weather and movement of seasons.

'Well,' said Derek. 'Their High Majesties over there seem happy enough with him. You're not going to say otherwise, are you?'

The Cluaracan studied us the way he'd studied the sky, then raised both arms straight out, the stick dangling from one, and gave a bow.

'To the victor the spoils,' he said. 'You will find it between blackened leaves, next to archaeology. Once you've located it, I'll have your next Feat for you. The craic will be mighty.'

Before we could respond, he turned and walked away.

Out on the water, two herons lifted themselves into the air, serenely, side by side, floating over the surface of the lake before settling down again, closer to the shore.

10.

REVENGE OF THE QUORUM

I HAD MANAGED to avoid dooming everybody to birdage with the successful Cycle. That was the first Feat down and only . . . three? Three to go? Oh geez.

'Okay, so the next thing on the festival agenda is the *ceilidh* tonight at eight,' Bob said. 'Uh, wait, do we have a quorum?'

A pale thing with sharp teeth sitting nearby raised an arm.

'What's a quorum, Tallykin?'

'A quorum, Doolin my friend, is a magical artifact of strange and mysterious power,' said an ancient-looking little fellow with a blue hat and a thin, curling beard that went down to his toes. 'I myself once defeated a ferocious borrabolga with a guardian quorum that hatched from the egg of a seven-headed serpent. Or was that a quail? I get the two mixed up.'

'A quorom is actually the minimum number of members required to be present for a committee meeting to be called to order,' said Helen, who had made a study of the arcane and mysterious rules of committee meetings and liked everyone to know it.

'I thought that was a gorgon?' said Tallykin. 'I spent a hundred years trapped in a committee meeting once. It only ended when a dragon got elected chair and ate everyone. It was such a relief.'

An impromptu emergency committee meeting had been convened in a corner of the Green. The Festival Committee was much reduced. Mum and Dad were *indisposed* and there was no sign of Sheila, who was back at the house baking more bread. Our quorum would have to remain a strange and mysterious thing of myth and legend. Bob was trying to work through an agenda, but Derek, Helen and me were far more concerned with puzzling out the Cluaracan's riddle to find the piece of the Cloak.

'Can he do that?' Derek demanded. 'Just talk gibberish like that? You won fair and square! There's no call for this sort of messin'!'

'Maybe it's traditional,' said Helen. 'You perform a Feat, you get a riddle. It probably seems perfectly obvious to him.'

I shook my head trying to shut them up, wracking my brains.

'Can we stick to the *ceilidh*, guys?' said Bob. 'This is important.'

On the podium, the hilarity had melted away from the royal faces like snow in sunlight, and they were wearing their stiff, scary masks again.

'Banshees on bikes! Can't you do anything right?' Tom Tracey called out.

'This whole thing is a complete shambles!' said Tricia Mulligan. 'Typical.'

Tricia and Tom glared at us, half angry, half mocking.

'Don't worry about the *ceilidh*,' said a voice from the ground. We looked down. The auld fella's little dog grinned up at us. The auld fella himself was standing a twine-length away. He gave a shy little wave. 'My man here will give them a swing around the floor the likes of which they'll never forget. And I guarantee that there'll be a few musicians from here around just gaspin' to play with him. Oh, it'll be a session that'll go down in history! We'll send 'em home sweatin' all right!'

He trotted off, taking the auld fella, who gave a high-pitched yip and kicked his heels, with him.

'Okay,' said Bob, relieved. 'Next there's the market in the morning . . .'

Market schmarket. All I could think about was the riddle. 'Between black leaves,' I said. 'Next to archaeology . . . it rings a bell, but I just can't . . .'

'Rubbish and nonsense!' declared Derek.

'I can't make head or tail of it,' admitted Helen, who had earlier declared that she was excellent at riddles.

But it did make sense, somehow, and I knew it made sense; I just couldn't remember what the sense was. Black leaves. You got black leaves in compost or mulch – is that what he meant? Archaeology. Did that refer to the crannog under the lake? Long Lisa's Tower? What? Maybe there was a big pile of mulched black leaves at the bottom of the Tower and the piece of the Cloak was under it?

'Focus, lads, focus!' said Bob. 'That's Brian's mum and

dad out there paddlin' in the shallows. They're depending on us!'

'We'll all be paddlin' if we're not careful,' muttered Derek.

'Good job there with them banshees, Brian,' Bob said. 'Very brave of you. Your mum and dad would be proud and they make a grand lookin' pair of herons, all the same. That is, I mean . . . '

'Don't worry about it,' I said. 'Look, Bob, if I said something was between black leaves and next to archaeology, what would you think?'

'I'd think this flippin' meeting was a waste of time, quorum or no quorum,' he said. 'Fine, I give up. Go read up on archaeology if that's how you want to pass your time. Let's just hope the Festival organises itself, shall we?'

'Ah, Dad,' said Derek. 'There's just the market tomorrow morning and the hurling match for the Under 13s and the beauty contest left on the Festival programme. They'll all happen like they always do.'

He was probably right. The market was just a table loaded down with Sheila's bread, and the hurling match was a weird non-event every year. The Under 13s would trot onto the field and wait for another team to show up. The other team never did, so it was declared a walkover Who were they supposed to be playing? No one seemed to know. It was just another odd tradition. I felt a tiny touch of unease. Maybe this year wouldn't be a walkover. Maybe this year there'd be another team on the pitch.

I shook my head. No. I had enough to worry about right now.

'I hate that beauty contest,' said Helen.

'Oh, dry up,' said Derek. 'It's just a bit of fun. I'll be at the match, and it'll be a walkover like usual. Mam's been makin' us bake that flippin' bread all month for the morning market, so there's no worries there.'

'Oh my God,' I said. *Go read up on archaeology.*

'I know!' said Helen. 'Let's just pretend the beauty contest isn't demeaning and sexist and horrible, shall we?'

'No, not that,' I said. 'I mean, yes, I agree – but look . . .'

I pointed across the Green, to the tiny spit of land and the building on the water that looked like a builder's hut slowly sinking into the mud.

'What?' said Derek, squinting. 'Is that the toilets?'

'No,' I said. 'It's the library. Come on. Let's go read up on archaeology.'

11.

THE SINKING LIBRARY

THE KNOCKMEALLDOWN TEMPORARY Public Library had been sitting crookedly on the edge of the world since the runaway pigs flattened the old library ten years before. Late at night a light sometimes came on inside, but nobody had borrowed a book from there in a long, long time. The worst of the mud might have been washed away since the Festival began, but the clean waters were lapping around it now, pushing gently against the rotting, flaking boards.

Helen led the way, marching up to the door and pressing her face as close to the filthy glass as she could without actually touching it.

'I think there's someone in there,' she said. 'I can just make them out. Oh wait, they've ducked down behind the table. Hello! I see you! Could you let us in, please? We just want to talk!'

Derek hammered on the door with a fist.

'Come on you crazy old bookworm, let us in! We're the Festival Committee and this is Festival business!'

I pulled him back before the door fell off its hinges, and we waited in silence. After what seemed like forever, a figure moved, rising from behind the table and shambling crookedly to the door. The lock clicked. The handle turned. The door opened slightly. A narrow, unfriendly, suspicious eye crept round the door as it opened and studied us.

'Since when do they let infants on the Committee?'

'Who else would be stupid enough?' said Derek.

'Are you the librarian?' I asked.

'By training and inclination, yes. However, since this rotting hovel and these empty shelves and these inane tomes could not possibly constitute a library, and since I haven't received a pay cheque in more years than I can count, I wouldn't go so far as to say that I am *the* librarian.'

'Jaykers, can you not give a straight flippin' answer?' said Derek.

'If it's straight answers you want, you need a library staffed by a properly employed professional librarian. Unless— Wait. *Wait.* Hang on a minute.'

The door was flung wide with a crash. One of its hinges fell off. The librarian, a pale man with a lined, pallid face and long greasy hair, was looking around wildly. 'Is that the *Great Festival*? Oh, lord, I lost track of the years! Oh my goodness, the Palace! Oh it is, it is!' He clapped his hands and jumped up and down with joy, then stopped, dismayed. 'But . . . but, surely the library . . . aren't they going to fix the library? Aren't they going to give me a new library full of books and periodicals and reference material? With a children's section full of beanie bags? And a space for historical displays and arts and crafts exhibitions? A staff room with a kettle and a coffee machine and tables and chairs and a nice view?'

He slumped down on the threshold, tears streaming down his face. Helen knelt down and patted him kindly.

'I'm sure you've been wonderful and done a fantastic job and they're sure to get around to rewarding you any minute now. In the meantime we were wondering if by any chance you had something on archaeology. Specifically, we're looking for the book next to a book on archaeology.'

He let us inside. The floor of the library was one big puddle, the tables and the shelves were rotting and the chairs appeared to have dissolved into the floor. There were sad piles of soggy books here and there, all fat with damp and stained with mildew and slime. Stained black. Black leaves, as in leaves of a book, as in pages. Derek kicked one, and there was an explosion of wet paper and cardboard. Helen growled at him as if he'd laughed out loud during a funeral.

'Archaeology's up there,' said the librarian from the doorway in a tired, timid voice. He pointed at a high shelf behind the desk where a single line of intact books were bravely preserved from the mud. Derek grabbed a rusty stepladder and leaned it against the shelf and I climbed it carefully, feeling the steps disintegrate under my feet as I went.

There. Alphabeticised and everything. Archaeology. And beside it, a bible, and all pages of the bible were all edged in black. And, like a bookmark between the pages, a roll of material covered in feathers.

I gently extracted the corner of the Cloak and held it up,

letting it fall open. It was soft to the touch, and the feathers shimmered like silk. Had the Cluaracan hidden it here all along? Or had he popped it in here during the Cycle just to give us an extra headache? Either way, we had it now. Fester would be—

Wait. Where was Fester?

The door of the library crashed inwards and fell apart in a shower of rotten clapboard. I nearly fell off the ladder. The Cluaracan sloshed in, water foaming around his boots.

'BRIAN NOLAN!' he roared.

'Excuse me!' said the librarian indignantly.

'ARE YOU BRIAN NOLAN?' The roar of the Cluaracan would have stripped the flesh of your bones. The librarian wilted under it like a loose page in a bonfire.

'No!' he squeaked.

'THEN GET OUT! What are you doing cooped up in here when there's a Festival on, anyway? Look at you, you're practically made of mildew! Out, out, out, enjoy yourself while you can!'

He chased the librarian out, then swung round and leaned on his stick, surveying us with a twinkle in his eye and a friendly grin on his face.

'Come in, come in, don't be shy!' he called behind him. Fester drooped in, every part of her slumped in sadness and defeat. 'We've been having a lovely chat, Fester and I. She's been telling me all about the things she's been telling you.'

'So what's the next Feat, then?' asked Helen belligerently, interrupting him. 'The *ceilidh*?'

'All right, dance-off!' said Derek and began throwing hip-hop shapes. 'Yo, I'm fixin' for some brawlin' with a leprechaun-a, I'll be getting' on it while he's rollin' on the lawn-a!'

'I'm not a leprechaun, you ignorant savage,' said the Cluaracan with a certain amount of stiff, wounded dignity. 'Yes, it is the *ceilidh*. But your Feat will be to kill the music.'

'Kill the music?' I said, bewildered. 'I like music! And I don't want to kill anything!'

'How do you kill music?' said Derek. 'Give it a bad review?'

'Don't be stupid!' said Helen. 'Music is immortal and can't be killed! It can't be done, I tell you! The music will live on!'

'But – wait, hang on, I don't understand,' I babbled anxiously and a little bit desperately. 'How am I supposed to do that?'

'You'd be like the conductor fella,' said Derek, waving his hands around. 'Get a big stick and beat it!'

'Stop that,' said the Cluaracan to Derek. 'How you go about it is up to you. Just try to keep time, and round it all off with a nice crescendo.'

'But – but it's music!' I said. 'You can't fight music! It's all just sound!'

'You can't stop the music!' yelled Helen. 'Nobody can stop the music!'

'They say music isn't the notes, but the silence in between,' said the Cluaracan with exaggerated patience. 'Just make it so it's all silence and no notes – the sound of silence if you like, then you won't feel so bad. Meanwhile, it's a beautiful day outside. You don't want to go wasting it stuck in here!'

He twirled his stick and twirled himself out the door, which was so full of bright sunlight it hurt to look at it from the gloomy shade of the library. Then he vanished into the brightness, leaving us blinking in the dark.

12.
THE *CEILIDH*

OUTSIDE, AGAINST ALL the odds, the Festival had started to be festive. The Junior Festival Committee were feeling about as festive as a famine.

We left the library in a bit of a daze. We had the rest of today to worry about tonight's Feat, to gnaw at it like a bone, for anxiety and tension to wind themselves into tighter knots in my stomach. I suppose I was relieved that he hadn't thrown me screaming head first into the next part of the Challenge, but a stay of execution only gives you more time to think about the firing squad cleaning their guns.

And, seriously? My Feat was to kill the music? Did that just mean pulling the plug on the *ceilidh*? Or was that too obvious, and too easy? He said kill the music, not cancel it. So let it start, then stop it? He had me thinking myself in knots. I was well and truly scuttered.

'Why the long faces?' said Fester. 'Take each moment as it comes! You won this one, Brian! You caught him on the hop and won a corner of the Cloak!'

'Yeah,' I said, untying my brain and unrolling the square

of material, the layers of feather stiff and soft, black and silver. 'Yeah, I did. Here, do you want it?'

I held it out to her but she leaped back with a squawk.

'No, Brian, no! Not while I'm still in his power! Oh make no mistake, while I'm here in your world I may be able to skirt around the charm because the gombeen never thought to extend it to humans, but he still holds me tight in an iron grip. If you give me the piece of the Cloak he will simply command me to give it to him, and it will be done.'

'Right,' I said, and folded it and put it away in a pocket. Fester assured me that I wouldn't damage the feathers.

'I flew for a year head first through a gale and not one of them feathers was so much as ruffled,' she said.

Gradually I began to feel lighter, easier. Tonight was tonight, today was today. Today had been a day like no other in my life, or anyone's life, and who knew what else was in store? If the remaining three Feats seemed impossible, well so had everything that had happened today, and they had happened anyway and here we were, still standing. The rest of the Cloak could be won, Mum and Dad could be given back to me, Fester freed, and everything made okay. So we took a bit of time off from being shocked and scared and worried and decided to be hopeful and optimistic instead. It was nice while it lasted.

Whatever else it had done, the Cycle had broken the ice, and the Folk had invited the people of Knockmealldown onto the promenades and platforms over the Lake. Now it was one long, happy, jolly, lively party. People and Folk sat and stood and ate and drank and chatted and sang. There was birdsong and the smells of good food cooking. The auld fella was somewhere, playing gentle music that was not sad, but content. We all twitched a bit at the sound, though, thinking about murder methods.

I suppose there was some magic at work somewhere. Whether it was the sort of magic you get from charms and spells or just the natural magic you get from people making the best of things, I don't know. I wondered if the Knockmealldowners had managed to forget about the threat, or not think about it for a while, or were pretending not to. They'd only get one chance in their lives to mingle with the Folk. Might as well take it while they could.

It was a long, lovely afternoon, stretching towards dinner and evening and nightfall. As it passed, I felt a weird mix of panic and relief. Time was moving on and so was the Festival. Every moment brought us closer to its end, but between now and then were all the things that had to go right. Was the first day of the Great Festival almost over already? Nearly. That meant the *ceilidh* was starting soon, and whatever the Cluaracan had planned with it. Herons at breakfast. Banshees at lunch. What was he going to do for dinner?

I stuck my hands in my pockets, and Derek, Helen, Fester and me wandered along the Green and sat down under a brave, thin tree that had somehow survived all the poisons and panics. We watched swans swimming on the bright blue water that had chased away the evil-smelling mud. Folk warriors with bronze weapons and shields were putting on a display, hacking at each other with swords and axes and spears, then sneakily shooting fireballs at each other. The Festival runs itself, I thought to myself. You don't have to worry so much.

'By the way, thank you for saving my life when I went flying off my bike,' I said to Fester. 'Or at least my bones.'

'Hate to see a man without his bones,' she said. 'Better in than out, as they say.'

'Would you do me a favour?' I handed her a stiff white envelope. 'Would you give that to the banshees?'

The envelope vanished into her feathers. 'I will. They can't see me, like the rest of the Folk, but I can slip it in one of their pockets. And what is it, might I ask?'

'Voucher for Una's Beauty Salon,' I said. 'It's supposed to be a prize for the raffle tomorrow night, but I thought they might like it.'

'You realise,' she said after a pause, 'that droppin' hints to a gang of supernatural terror women that they need a trip to the Beauty Salon might not be the smartest thing in this world or any other?'

'Oh,' I said 'Oh. Maybe I'd better—'

'Too late!' she held up a wing. 'We'll just have to see what they do.'

We went onto the Floating Palace and wandered the walks and ways. Folk performers juggled with impossible things like sofas and cars and globs of water. A rock-troll sat at a table, sprinkled salt and pepper over a shiny scimitar and daintily nibbled it away to nothing, dabbing his mouth with a white napkin, which he then ate along with the table and the chair.

Derek's pals from the hurling team roared past with their shirts off and tribal patterns painted all over their pale white torsos, whooping and hollering, but they didn't bother anyone and nobody bothered them. The banshees on their bikes went carefully through the crowds without their feet ever touching the ground. Everybody gave them respectful space, but nobody ran away screaming.

It seemed to go on forever. Every step brought a new sight to see and a new sound to hear. It seemed like days passed in the long afternoon. Every moment was full to the brim, not just with things and sights and sounds but with the feeling of freedom and summer and friends, sometimes lazy and sometimes so full of energy the top your head seemed to fizz and bubble. And then you realised the air itself was fizzing and bubbling.

But time did pass. And eight o'clock neared, and with it the *ceilidh*. I tried to prepare myself, to brace myself. Should I clear my head or fill it full of plans and tactics? I couldn't do either. My brain was full of too many thoughts and none of them seemed useful.

The air cooled, and the sun's light turned into a gentle rosy glow. Insects rose from the grass and the water, but they were herded by tiny Folk, and nobody was bitten and nobody had to slap them off their arms or shake them out of their hair. The insects hung in clouds, and as the light of the sun faded, they began to shine green and yellow and red and purple.

Every Knockmealldowner who had ever held an instrument wanted to have a go. They got up and they played on the pavilion, and there was a little bit of singing and dancing. The music was fun and lively, and some of it was lovely and haunting. Gradually everybody moved towards the Tower. The auld fella was going to play, and then the real session would start. All the other musicians crowded around the pavilion, leaving a reverential space for the auld fella.

It was time for the *ceilidh*.

I braced myself. Get this over with. There'd be war, but I had no choice.

'I'm going to do it,' I said, trying to sound decisive. 'I'm going to announce it's cancelled.'

'There'll be war,' said Derek. 'This'll be brilliant!'

'It's wrong!' said Helen. 'The music didn't do anything to anybody! The music is innocent!'

The auld fella shook hands and chatted with the other musicians, and the little dog hopped down off the platform.

I took a deep breath, then it occurred to me that there was no sign of the Cluaracan. We hadn't seen him since the library. I started to panic. So long as I couldn't see him, he could be up to anything.

'Where is he?' I said. 'Where is he?'

'Probably tryin' to get that harp string into that egg and then the egg into that eagle,' said Derek. 'With a bit o' luck the eagle ate him.'

'Maybe you should stand on a chair?' suggested Helen. 'And we could find you a megaphone or something?'

I opened my mouth to say something sarcastic, but then I realised that this was actually a really good idea.

'Chair and a megaphone,' I muttered, looking around.

'All right?' said the dog. He had wound his way through the legs of the crowd to reach us. The blue twine that attached him to the auld fella stretched impossibly between them.

'Yeah,' I said. 'You?'

'Not too bad. We should have a grand old hoolie for ourselves tonight, hey?'

'Uh. Yeah. Maybe. I just can't help feeling worried.'

'Worried?' said the dog. 'Why should you be worried? Kick back and relax! Everyone's having the time of their lives! Even the herons and swans! So throw some shapes and bash your brogues with the rest of 'em!'

Nobody, human, swan or heron, would be bashing their brogues or throwing any sort of shapes tonight if I had my way, but I tried to smile, and said I would.

'Brian?' said Helen.

'Yeah?'

'What are you doing?'

'Doing? I'm just talking with the . . . with the . . .' Why was she looking at me like that? As if I'd suddenly sprouted a second head? 'With . . . I'm just talking!'

'No,' said Derek. 'Not here. What are you doing over *there*?'

Over there, on the podium, the auld fella was reluctantly handing his fiddle over to a young boy who had asked to hold it. The boy had a big friendly smile, and his eyes were alight with admiration and enthusiasm. He was wearing boots and combat trousers and a t-shirt, and his head was shaved. Except for the friendly smile and the eyes alight with admiration and enthusiasm, he was me.

'That's me,' I said, pointing at the me that was examining the fiddle, testing its balance, putting it under my chin, pretending to play. The auld fella reached for it anxiously. I gave a little laugh and handed it back. It slipped from my hand and dropped towards the ground. With reflexes that were definitely not mine, that weren't even the reflexes of some of the faster striking snakes, I caught it again, went 'phew!' and handed it back to the auld fella, who was on the verge of a heart attack.

'Oh no,' said the dog.

'Oh no what?' I said. 'Who is that? What happened? What did I do? That wasn't me! I didn't do that! WHO AM I?'

'Listen, kid,' said the dog. 'Word of advice. I think I know what's going to happen, and if I'm right you're going to need gravemoss, okay? Gravemoss. Good luck. Hey! Stop! Stop! Don't play!'

The dog shot towards the pavilion, barking and shouting. Too late. The auld fella raised his bow and his fiddle to play the first note. The me on the pavilion poked something in his ears and jumped off the stage and was lost in the crowd. The last I saw of him was a swirl of feathers.

'That's the one!' I said. 'That guy that's me is the Cluaracan! Listen! Everybody! This *ceilidh* is cancelled! Due to unfortunate unforeseen circumstances! LISTEN TO ME!'

It was too late. They were listening, but not to me, and I wasn't even listening to myself. The music already had me. A wild sudden fever was burning in me, wiping away all thoughts of the Cluaracan and the Challenge and the Feat. Forgetting Mum and Dad and the Cloak and everything, I jumped in the air and started to dance.

13.

GRAVEMOSS

THE FIRST SCRAPE, the first note, lit a fire in every heart that heard it.

The second note sent blood rushing to every limb.

The third exploded in every brain like a firework.

By the time the auld fella played the fourth we were all dancing, dancing, dancing, and every musician was playing, playing, playing. The music was everywhere, in every ear, in every leg, in every arm, and everybody danced, everybody reeled and jigged and hornpiped. Babies too small to do anything other than wriggle danced in their parent's arms. People in wheelchairs waved their arms over their heads and did wheelies.

'Look at me!' yelled Derek. 'I'm dancin'! I'm the lord o' the dance!'

'If you want to call that dancing,' said Fester, her beak fluttering like a yellow ribbon in a breeze.

'Go Derek!' yelled Helen, and the four of us swung in and out, round and round, arm in arm together.

All across the Floating Palace people and Folk joined hands and danced round in great rings, raising arms, dancing under and through, and the rings mixed together in huge dancing knots. The King danced dainty little steps and the Queen kicked her legs high. The insect lights swirled and mixed. Cheers rose with the stars and howled at the moon. Everyone danced, danced, danced, lost in the music, lost in the movement, lost in the happiness. Joy was on every face. Feet kicked, arms flapped, sweat flew, bodies were thrown and caught, flipped and somersaulted.

'This is incredible!' Helen shouted as we joined a long line of people doing the can-can.

'It's like my legs have minds of their own!' I shouted back.

'You've more brains in your feet than in your heads anyway!' said Fester.

'Look at it go!' Derek laughed as he kicked high and one of his runners flew off, sailing majestically into the lake.

The musicians played and played, one tune melting into another and another without pause or let. Dancing men and women and Folk brought them food and drinks they gulped down between notes. Their instruments steamed in the cooling night air. Their fingers bled, their lungs ached, their arms burned, and still they played and they played and they played.

'Is this the Siege Of Ennis?' asked Helen as we moved through rings of people, going from partner to partner in a complicated pattern.

'The Walls of Limerick, maybe?' I said. We were all breathless and panting and sweating.

'In a place called Knockmealldown!' crowed Derek. 'It's really a heck of a town! They love dancin' all night, till dawn's early light, just watch 'em go round and round!'

'Not sure that rhymes,' Fester said, but not so loud Derek could hear.

Hours passed, and hours and hours, and the dancing and the playing went on without rest or break, as happy and joyful as at the very first note. But the bodies were sorer and heads were lighter, eyes were blurring and throats were raw with singing and yelling. Up and down the walkways and the platforms and the bridges, feet thumping on the wooden boards, in line after line all along the railings.

'This is fun and all,' said Helen as we waved our arms in the air as if we just didn't care. 'But are we going to take a break soon?'

'I'm gaspin' for a bit of hydration!' said Derek.

'Why would you want to ever stop?' I cried.

'We can dance forever!' said Fester.

The moon crossed the sky from one side to the other in a graceful gavotte, and the stars turned in vast galactic waltzes. I was whirling with Fester, round and round and up and down, waltzing and jiving and tangoing. Dances long forgotten came back to us, dances we never knew. I was grinning, everything forgotten, happier than I'd ever been in my life. Fester's eyes were shining as if she was remembering how to be happy after long years of sadness. Sometimes the thought came to me that I was supposed to kill the music, and I laughed. What a terrible thought! Why would anyone want the music to stop?

We didn't notice how tired we were. We didn't notice that the night and the dance seemed to have no end.

Until Lackley caught us.

Fester and me were whirling together when the cow slid out of the crowd and trapped us between her wide snowy flank and a tall wooden railing. She wasn't dancing, though she was tapping her hooves. We were still dancing but we had no way to get out past her. Standing straight as rods, we riverdanced side by side.

'YOU'VE GOT TO STOP THIS!' roared Lackley. 'OR IT'LL NEVER STOP AT ALL! ALL THE HUMANS HERE WILL KEEP DANCING UNTIL THEY DIE! YOU HAVE TO STOP THE MUSIC!'

She pulled away and let us through. My mind came back to itself with a jolt, even though my body did not. Fester's feathers shivered as she woke up and looked around, shocked. We hopped and kept hopping, the rhythm of the music inside us like a living thing. I can't be dancing, I can't be dancing, I can't be dancing. The thought whirling round in my brain, but like every other part of me, it was dancing too. I had to stop, I had to stop the music. I had to stop.

I grabbed Fester by the wing and together we dodged and ducked and bounced and slid away, off the Floating Palace, across the Green, through the dim dark shadows full of twitching tendrils in the Ghost Pig Estate, onto the road and up the street.

'Where are we going?' Fester asked, sounding as groggy and confused as I felt. We were reeling as we reeled.

'Gravemoss!' I said. 'The little dog said we'd need gravemoss!'

'Oh! Of course. That'll do it.'

Our arms and legs and hands and bodies moved of their own accord. I kept pushing, leaning, fighting to go up. Up the hill, up the street to the only place I could think of where I might find something called gravemoss.

'The Cluaracan put a spell on the fiddle, the rotten soak!' Fester said.

'But why did he look like me?'

'To create confusion and mischief!'

'Well it worked!'

The music followed us the whole way, as loud and alive as if we were standing right next to it. Hand in wing, swinging together, up to the church, down to the gap between the church and the priest's house, down into the dark, through the rusted old gate, into the graveyard.

During the day, the graveyard looked like the ruins of an ancient dwarven city, with weather-worn blocks lying at every angle in the mossy humps that bubbled up from under the surface. The ground was soft and yielding amongst the broken tombs and fallen gravestones, and we tripped and stumbled as we danced in the dark.

'Okay, we just need to find some moss!' I said. I didn't have to yell to be heard any more, but my mouth and throat were dry as a desert and even my tongue felt nearly too tired to talk.

'No shortage of that,' said Fester. 'Wait a minute though. What in the name of Macnas is going on here?'

The graveyard was full of snapping and cracking sounds, like spoons being struck together hard and fast. There were white things amongst the graves, flying around, clicking and clacking together. A skull rolled across the air, grinning. It was caught by a skeleton hand and thrown back to land in a skeleton ribcage. There were bones everywhere, capering around their own graves and headstones.

'Never mind them, Brian!' said Fester. 'Get what we came here for!'

I grabbed handfuls of moss off an ancient grave and stuffed it in my ears until I couldn't hear the music any more. It was still there, a throbbing deep inside that made me twitch and tremble, but the dancing stopped. I nearly collapsed. God, my body was so tired. And I was surrounded by dancing bones and skeletons. Okay.

I chased after Fester to stuff moss in her ears. They were big and bat-like and took a lot of stuffing. The moss kept falling out, and her hearing was so acute we needed handful after handful before the music cut out for her, too. When it finally did we sat down on the edge of a grave, sweating, sore and out of breath.

'We have,' I gasped. 'We have to stop that flippin' music!'

'What?' said Fester. We were both deaf from the gravemoss.

'We have to stop the flippin' music!' I shouted.

'That must be a charm of endless playing and endless dancing the Cluaracan put on the auld fella's fiddle!' she shouted back. 'Almost impossible to break without doing somethin' injurious to the player!'

With a groan, I stood up and forced my complaining limbs to at least think about considering the idea of starting to walk.

'We can't do anything from up here, anyway!' I said.

'We'd better get back to the Pond. Here, let's grab more of this moss! We can get a few others to help.'

'There won't be enough for everyone,' said Fester as we stuffed our pockets. 'And it's the fiddle and the fiddler we need to stop!'

'We could rush him?' I suggested. 'Grab the fiddle off him?'

'If you get too close you'll just start dancin' again, even with half a graveyard's worth of moss in your ears! It gets into your bones!'

Speaking of bones, the dancing skeletons had all vanished, which was a relief because they were incredibly creepy and strange.

'Come on!' I said. 'Let's go. We'll think of something. We'll break the charm, perform the Feat, win the piece of Cloak and we really need to do it all before someone has a heart attack or something. They don't call 'em Feats for nothing do they?'

'No need for feets at all! Hang on!'

Fester spread her wings, flapped, and took off. It never occurred to me that she *could* fly. If you could call what she did flying. Technically, she was airborne, and she was even able to grab hold of my shoulders with her claws and lift me up, ignoring my kicking and screaming. With her wings flapping furiously and weighed down by a struggling me, it was the flying equivalent of rolling at full speed down an old bog road in a gale force wind at midnight during a rock concert.

'Not so tight!' I wailed. 'Your claws are ripping my shoulders off! It hurts!'

'Why don't I let go and see how much that hurts?'

We bounced and jounced and bucked and veered as Fester struggled to go in something vaguely like a straight line, swinging me to the left and the right as if I were a counterweight on a clock, rattling my teeth, banging my legs off walls and trees and houses and chimneys. I screamed a lot, but thanks to the moss in her ears Fester probably couldn't hear much of it so that was okay.

The skeletons were below. They were all lined up along the path, from the graveyard to the road and down Main Street, dancing up and down with that terrible rattling, bones flying away from them and swinging back, the happiest bunch of bones I'd ever seen, and also the most terrifying. A crowd of them were congregating around somebody's house – I couldn't be sure whose because I was trying not to get smeared across the guttering – and the skeletons were now passing things back along the line, juggling small round objects from skeletal hand to skeletal hand.

'What are they doing down there?' I asked.

'I've enough on me mind without worryin' about a bunch o' boney weirdos!' Fester squawked.

We passed over Ghost Pig Estate, the houses dark and brooding and full of malice, then over the Green and the Floating Palace and the crowds of dancing Folk and people and the moonlit water and the glowing insects.

'Here we go!' screeched Fester.

She flapped hard as Long Lisa's Tower loomed over us. Through the side of the pavilion I could see the auld fella, playing ecstatically, surrounded by musicians and dancers and dancing musicians. They all looked ready to drop, grey-faced and slack-jawed, eyes drooping, shoulders slumping, but they had to keep moving, moving, moving. They'd been going non-stop for hours and hours now. How much longer could they keep it up?

Fester struggled to lift us up to the height of the pavilion. 'Higher!' I yelled. 'Up, up!'

'Try flappin' your arms instead of your mouth and see if that helps!'

Even through the gravemoss in my ears, the music was starting to beat and scrape and swing, far-off and muffled. My muscles all started to twitch and I could feel Fester trying to fly to the rhythm.

The roof of the pavilion was not low, but the floor was packed with bodies big and small and we were too long to fit in the space between all those bobbing heads and the ceiling. I lifted my legs as high as I could and Fester ducked low, flapping and veering. All the pale faces stared up at us in astonishment even as their poor exhausted bodies jigged on. The air in there was hot and stale, smelling of sweat and B.O. and athlete's foot. A huge set of curling horns snagged my feet and we were dead in the air until I kicked free, apologising to the goat-thing I sent falling to the floor.

'There he is!' I pointed at the auld fella. 'Aim for him!'

'You try aimin' for something with a ten ton weight hangin' off you!'

I could feel myself starting to dance as we closed in on the auld fella, my whole body jerking and bouncing. The auld fella was playing in a joyful delirium, the little dog jumping up and down at his feet. There was nothing I could do. It was in me, again, and in Fester.

I wriggled my right shoulder out of Fester's claws, letting one arm swing free, and as we passed the auld fella I reached for the fiddle, desperately stretching and straining, fighting the notes that were worming their way through the moss and into my brain, making me forget, carrying me away into a never-ending dream of music and dance that wouldn't end until my body gave up and fell down dead.

With a discordant scrape, the music died.

'Got it! Got it! Aagh don't let go!'

The fiddle was in my hand. I waved it around so Fester could see it. We'd done it! We could stop! My left shoulder was slipping out of her claws!

I nearly clubbed a few confused people with the fiddle, but Fester saw and she grinned and she went in to land. And she missed. We flew out through the other side of the pavilion.

'Go back! Go back!' I yelled.

'I can't! I can't!' she screeched, wings flapping desperately.

I could see the dense jungle of thorns that crowded around the base of the Tower. I screamed. It didn't matter. Fester couldn't go any further. We had stopped flying and started falling.

Up on the pavilion, the rest of the musicians faltered, all suddenly slumping where they sat or stood. Their instruments fell from their numb fingers with a clatter and a jangle. All over the Floating Palace the dancers came to a stop, puffing and panting. Suddenly all their soreness and their tiredness crashed down on them. They fell on the boards and the benches and tables or curled up on the grass of the Green, too utterly exhausted to even crawl to a bed or find somewhere comfortable.

Nobody spoke a word. The air was full of the groans and moans of aching tiredness. Then it filled with people's slow, heavy breathing as they slipped off into a deep dreamless sleep, Folk and humans lying side by side. None of them heard the splash as Fester and me fell, kicking, screaming, in a long, sickening arc that carried us over the hawthorns and the shore of the isle and into the waters of the Lake of Lisashee.

Once I was over the sudden shock of wet and cold, which was actually very welcome on my worn-out, sore and sweaty body, I started to swim. Mum and Dad had been teaching me since before I could even walk. I'd done lifesaving courses and everything. Either Fester couldn't swim, or her wings were too utterly worn out to even try. She was thrashing and drowning a few yards away.

As I struck out for Fester, I had to let the auld fella's fiddle slip out of my heand, and it sank to join the marquee and the Crannog and the dinosaur bones, all lost deep in the mud of the lake. Then I grabbed her by the handful of sodden feathers on the scruff of her neck and dragged her back to the shore.

It wasn't far, and after half a minute there was solid mud under our feet and we could crawl, gasping like a pair of dying steam engines, onto the dry sandy strip between the water and the thorns – the same place, more or less, where Mulkytine had cornered the Junior Festival Committee the day before.

We sat, panting, and watched as the lights faded, all the glowing insects drifting away to their own beds, and nothing was moving anywhere, not even a ripple on the water. We listened to the swelling silence.

'We did it,' I said.

Fester's only reply was a faint squeak.

It seemed unreal. The *ceilidh* had been a huge, roaring, living thing, and we'd made it all go quiet. We'd done it.

'The second Feat,' I said, my voice fading, my eyes drooping. 'The second part of the Challenge. In your face, Cluaracan.'

Half the Cloak was ours.

We flopped down on our backs, and were asleep before our heads hit the ground.

Part Three:
Sunday

1.

THE STOLEN BREAKFAST

I WOKE UP between two herons.

I was lying stiff and sore on the little beach, and they stood like guardians on either side, their beaks crossed above me.

'Mum?' I said. 'Dad?'

When I moved and sat up, they spread their wings, bent their legs, jumped into the air and swam into the sky, drifting back over the lake, and settling down at the centre of two expanding ripples that spread across the surface of the water and faded gently into stillness.

I was groggy, rubbing my eyes, wondering if it was a dream, wondering if it had all been a dream. The Floating Palace was still there, though, stretching out from the Isle, and sleeping bodies lay all over the place, like snoring leftovers after a messy picnic. The sun was high. We'd slept late. I was aching and thirsty and hungry. My clothes were still damp, and they'd chilled me. I needed a hot shower and breakfast and a week in bed.

Fester was curled up in a little ball of feathers and rags, snoring gently through her long yellow beak. Her wings were going to be in an awful state today. Poor Fester.

The sleepers on the Floating Palace were beginning to stir and wake, blinking the dew from their eyes. They sat up and they stretched, working the aches and the kinks from their muscles, sore from the dancing and from sleeping on rocks or roads or in funny shapes, shivering a little from the cool of the ground. Then a baby began complaining and looking for food, and soon so did everyone else.

Further up the little beach there was a wooden staircase spiralling up over the thorns to the pavilion. I shook Fester gently a few times, but she rolled over and muttered something about using my guts to make spaghetti bolognese if I didn't shove off and leave her alone, so I did that, and climbed the stairs wearily to the pavilion. There were bodies everywhere. Stepping carefully, I made my way over to the podium in the middle with the thrones, where the auld fella was sleeping blissfully, the little dog on his lap.

The King and the Queen, who had slept in the middle of the crowd, both suddenly sat up, clothes and hair askew, looking as undignified and unregal as everyone else.

'Breakfast,' said the Queen. 'Where is the Festival Bread?'

'Where's the boy?' demanded the King. Standing on the podium, I was higher than everyone else and hard to miss. His voice sounded strangely muffled and distant. I could barely make out what he was saying. 'There you are! Approach!'

We both looked at the yawning, groaning mess of people and Folk between us.

'Er, no, stay there, actually. Clear the way! Clear the way!'

The King and the Queen climbed over and around bleary-eyed, scratching, mumbling, squinting bodies until they reached the podium. They didn't tower over me. I was only a little bit shorter than them, though the antlers made them seem bigger. They looked at me with their strange, sad, angry eyes. I didn't particularly like them and for a moment I felt like sneering at them. They had turned my parents into herons, after all. For Fester's sake, though, I had to try to be nice. Also, they were terrifying and could turn me into things if I annoyed them too much.

'Good morning,' I said, then added: 'Your Majesties.'

'Good morning, Brian Nolan,' said the King, still sounding as if he were a very long way away. 'You have moss growing out of your ears. Is that what young humans are into nowadays?'

'What? Oh!' I pulled the moss from my ears and then tilted my head first one way and then the other to let the water pour out.

'So, um, did you . . . have a good time?' I asked finally. 'Last night?'

'There was fine music and fine dancing last night,' said the King.

'For a while we forgot our troubles and cares,' said the Queen.

'Oh,' I said, and was about to say 'good!' Then it occurred to me that two people who were missing their daughter might not be terribly happy about forgetting her, even for a short while. They looked at me gravely.

'Well,' said the King finally. 'There's no denying the sport and entertainment that filled the first day of the Great Festival, despite the poor start.'

'Should this continue,' said the Queen, 'you will find us grateful and generous.'

'Thank you,' I squeaked. 'But I just want my mum and dad back the way they were.'

The King and the Queen looked at each other, a little shamefaced.

'Perhaps we . . . over-reacted,' said the King. 'Though we were provoked. Others have suffered more for doing less, but this is Knockmealldown and the Great Festival. Your parents will be returned to human form.'

'After breakfast,' said the Queen.

A bubble of pure happiness rose inside me.

'Oh thank you, thank you, thank you! Thank you! Thank you!'

They kept staring at me and I kept saying thank you until it started to get a bit weird and I stopped. They kept staring at me.

'Uh, breakfast?' I said.

'Yes,' said the King.

'You may bring it before us,' said the Queen.

'Bring what?' I said.

'Breakfast!' said the King testily. 'This is the second day of the Festival is it not? Where is the Festival bread?'

'The what?'

'The black bread,' said the Queen. 'Of the Festival.'

I felt my eyes go round and my jaw drop open.

'Oh,' I said. 'Oh. Oh! The bread! You mean Sheila's

bread! For the market! Wait. Just wait right there. Derek! Helen! Fester! Help! We need bread! Sheila's bread!'

Without waiting for anyone else, I ran pell-mell out of the pavilion and down steps and over bridges and along boardwalks. The Bellamore house was packed to the rafters with her inedible bread. Breakfast bread for the Good Folk! All we had to do was get it down to the Green and everybody'd be happy! I was bouncing with excitement. Sheila's bread! Mum and Dad! Sorted!

I saw Derek and Helen tripping and staggering towards me, and Bob and Tom and Tricia helping each other to their feet. We all met at a wide, open platform. Before I could explain, a small human woman came roaring off the Green in a fury.

'Sheila?' said Bob as she reached the platform. 'Are you all right?'

'It's gone!' Sheila shrieked in rage, coming to a stop. 'It's all gone! Every last bit of it! I finished the last batch just before the *ceilidh* started and then I was dancing with everyone else for ages and ages and then when it finished I just fell asleep sitting up against the tree over there, and when I woke up I went home because I knew we'd need the bread for the Festival Breakfast – but it was all gone! Somebody stole all my bread!'

I opened my mouth and a tiny faint wail of horror and disbelief came out.

'Your bread?' said Tom with a laugh. 'Why would *anyone* steal your bread?'

'Sheila,' said Bob, steering her towards a bench, 'I know that bread means a lot to you, but why don't you sit down there and relax yourself and as soon as we've got a bit of breakfast sorted for the Good Folk we'll find your bread, okay?'

'Bob,' said Sheila. 'You're an idiot! We need to find that bread NOW!'

Derek snorted. 'Geez, calm down, Ma. It's only manky old bread nobody can eat. Who cares?'

'It's their breakfast,' I said faintly, then, louder: 'Their breakfast is the bread! I mean the bread is their breakfast! It's the Festival Breakfast!'

'They want to *eat* Sheila's bread?' asked Bob in disbelief. 'Sheila's bread's not for eatin'; it's for paperweights or bookends or repairin' old stone walls. Nobody *eats* it. Er. Sorry, Sheila.'

'Oh dear,' said Fester from behind me. She was pulling long lengths of dripping moss out of her ears. 'This is a problem. That manky old bread you speak of so disrespectfully isn't just any old tasteless human loaf. The secret bread of Knockmealldown is a great delicacy to the Good Folk, a delicacy they only get to taste once every hundred years. You really had better find that bread and find it fast.'

Into the shocked silence that followed came the Cluaracan, and behind him the King and Queen. Hungry-looking Folk crowded around, looking for their Festival bread.

'At this rate, we'll be having breakfast for supper,' said the Cluaracan heartily. 'It was a wild old night last night, but surely a few loaves of bread shouldn't be too difficult to procure?'

'Uh, there's a small problem with that, Your Majesties,' said Bob.

'Explain yourselves!' barked the King.

'The bread is missing,' I said. 'It's been stolen.'

A gasp of horror went through the crowd of Folk. One started to wail. The others grumbled and growled and hissed.

'Stolen?' said the Queen. 'Who would dare?'

'Are you saying,' said the Cluaracan, 'that, under cover of last night's *ceilidh*, the Festival bread of Knockmealldown was taken away and hidden, if not destroyed? I doubt it will ever be seen again! Your Majesties, this is a disgrace!'

'Wait a minute,' I said. 'There was something going on down on the street when we flew over . . .'

'Now that I think of it,' said the Cluaracan, turning a piercing gaze on me. 'There was something enchanted about last night's revels, wasn't there? And wasn't it yourself I saw interfering with the musician's fiddle before the start? Could it be that you were hoping to hold the bread hostage against the return of your parents? That is low cunning indeed, Master Nolan, and not in the spirit of Festival!'

I reeled backwards under the onslaught.

'Thief!' someone in the crowd cried. 'Where's our bread?'

'Now, now,' said Bob. 'I'm sure all this can be cleared up if we just calm down.'

The King drew himself up. Bob quailed before the tiny figure.

'We are long-lived and far-travelled,' said the King. 'We

live under the earth and between the sky and water. We weave cloth from moonbeams, drink nectar from the sun. But there are few things as dear to us as the breakfast we receive on the morning of the second day of the Great Festival of Knockmealldown. Without it, there can be no Great Festival, and with no Great Festival there is no bond of goodwill between us. Brian Nolan, representative of the Knockmealldown Festival Committee, WHERE IS OUR BREAKFAST?'

'We don't know!' wailed Sheila.

Groans of disappointment and grief came from the Folk. Every single shoulder slumped, every head drooped, every lower lip protruded and every eye quivered and blinked and every nose sniffed. It was unbearable.

'Listen to me!' I said. 'Please! Give us a chance to look for it!'

'I beg your pardon,' said the Queen. 'Perhaps some of your moss got in my ears. Did you say something?'

The King rounded on me.

'Find it and have it brought before us,' he said. It was a cool, aloof command. A royal decree. He held out his arm and the Queen joined him. 'You have one hour. Cluaracan?'

'One hour it is, your majesty,' said the Cluaracan.

'If we have not been served in that time then we'll make birds of every last one of them,' said the Queen.

'An hour,' said the King, and they proceeded back towards the Isle, and the Folk all followed, some sad, some angry, some puzzled. The Cluaracan remained. He leaned over and spoke to me softly.

'Enjoy your final hour. Savour your achievement. Two Feats isn't bad, you know. I wouldn't go so far as to call it heroic. It almost rises to adequate, perhaps. But even so, I suspect the rest of your sad life will be downhill from here, forever reliving the brief glory days when you completed two Feats and won two pieces of a ratty old Cloak from a kindly old man who was going easy on you. So really, this is all for the best. Even if you were to find the bread, it is well guarded. Tell you what, when you fail, you can be a bird with the rest of 'em. I'll even make you a heron so you can be a happy family again.'

I glared at him.

'Is it a Feat?' I said.

He hesitated, eyes calculating.

'Oh come on,' I said. 'If this is it, if this is the thing that'll mean we're all turned into birds, then make it a Feat. If you're so certain I'll fail, then why not? I'm pretty sure you were planning to steal the bread all along anyway. You're doing everything you can to wreck the Festival.'

He narrowed his eyes and spoke with a sly hiss.

'Oh, I mean to destroy this Festival once and for all. You are correct about that, little boy. Did sweet little Fester tell you how she ended up in her current hilarious form?'

'She said you chased her and caught her and stole her Cloak.'

'Ah, but *why* was I chasing her? She came out of the Otherworld to investigate the troubling tidings coming from Lisashee. The bulldozers ploughing and the diggers digging. She saw it all, the ugly destruction of the beautiful lakeside by human hands and human machines; but it was her misfortune that she also saw me, in human guise, amongst the humans, and more her misfortune that I saw her. I couldn't let her escape back to the Otherworld and tell the Good Folk that I had grown to hate Knockmealldown so much I conspired with humans to completely ruin a place that was sacred to us, bringing the anger of the Folk down on the village. This weekend is the final nail in Knockmealldown's coffin. Do not get in my way.'

'Why?' I said, aghast. It all sounded like nothing but spiteful meanness to me; destroying something lovely for no good reason. 'Why are you doing this?'

His resentful, ruddy face softened for a moment. His eyes went distant and far-away.

'It was here she rejected me, child. One hundred years ago she laughed in my face when I asked for her hand. The whole Festival witnessed it, and found it most amusing. You see, child, one day she will come round. One day she will see that I love her more than anyone ever could and I will give her everything she could possibly want. But until that day, this Festival burns like gall in my heart. Let it die. Let all of Knockmealldown vanish into the air and be forgotten. Then maybe she'll take more care how she speaks to me.'

'You're mad,' I said.

'No,' he said. 'In love. Easy mistake to make. You have fifty minutes. You'll enjoy life as a bird. It's very carefree.'

'Is it a Feat?' I repeated. 'My next Feat. To serve the Festival Breakfast. Is it a Feat?'

The Cluaracan growled in frustration, rolled his eyes

and gave a curt nod. He walked away and left me standing there with my ears ringing and my eyes watering. It's hard not to get upset when a bully who despises you for no good reason, who's bigger, stronger and smarter than you, pummels you with their words and their pure hate, and promises to destroy you.

'You owe me that piece of the Cloak, by the way!' I called after his retreating back, my voice cracking a little. 'I murdered the music for you! Before it murdered us! In case you've forgotten!'

He waved a hand at me over his shoulder, but kept walking.

'Brian,' said Helen. 'What are we going to do? We need to find that bread, now!'

'C'mon, Brian,' said Derek. 'Tell us you have a plan!'

'Funnily enough,' I said, sniffing and wiping my eyes. 'I think I do.

'You all right, Brian?' said Helen, putting a hand on my shoulder. Derek was squinting at me curiously. I took a deep, gulping breath and nodded.

'Yeah,' I said. 'Thanks. Come on. I think I know where the bread is. I also think we'll have a hard time getting it back without some help.'

'Help?' Derek looked puzzled. 'What help? Who?'

'I forgot in all the excitement,' I said. 'Last night Fester and me were flying over the street, and I saw the skeletons stealing the bread out of the house. Flippin' skeletons.'

'Skeletons?' said Helen. 'Skeletons stole the bread? Were they hungry? Poor things.'

'Thievin' bags o' bones!' said Derek. 'That's *our* rotten manky bread! Wait. You were flyin'?'

'But I just had this mad idea,' I said. 'About who might be able to help us get it back.'

I walked past them, past the Committee, past Knockmealldowners blinking with bleary confusion. I walked into Ghost Pig Estate until I was standing in front of our house. Helen and Derek followed, slowly, hesitantly.

'Hello?' I called out. 'Are you there?'

I felt stupid and foolish. The Knockmealldowners were all looking at me as if I'd lost my head completely.

I felt a feathered hand take mine. I looked down into her cave-like eyes.

'Now this is a good idea,' Fester said. 'Why didn't I think of it?'

'You've a lot on your mind,' I said. I raised my eyes and looked into the Estate.

'Help!' I called. 'I need your help! I never really believed in you before, but I do now! Please, help me! Help my mum and dad! I know Knockmealldown was cruel to you, but you helped me, didn't you? You trampled the Hëlweed. Please, help me now!'

The houses and the Hëlweed swallowed the sound of my voice, eating my words. It was like shouting at a wall. They died, and there was silence, deathly, dull and flat. Then I heard a far-off sound, like drumming, and a cloud of dust began to rise amongst the haunted houses.

2.

PIGS AND BONES

I LED THE way to the graveyard. The Committee and the rest of the Knockmealldowners bunched up behind me, looking nervously back over their shoulders as we climbed the winding way up Main Street. The crooked old houses seemed to twist in towards us or lean away from us, roofs like cocked hats that reminded me of the Cluaracan. There were no Folk about, except for Fester, jogging beside me. They'd retreated to Long Lisa's Tower and wrapped it in a white mist. The hour was ticking down.

I hurried up the hill, crossed the road and went down the narrow overgrown path between the Church and the priest's house, to the gap and the graveyard with the broken headstones, shattered tombs and humps of moss and grass. There were no dancing skeletons there now. Maybe they'd gone back to their rest, I thought hopefully. Perhaps for another hundred years, perhaps just until next Halloween?

Left lying in great piles on the graves, rocks, tombs and humps were heaps and piles of small, round, black rolls.

'Quick!' I yelled. 'Grab the bread and get back to the Green! Quick, before—'

Click-clack-clatter-crack. Bones erupted from mossy graves and broken tombs. Leg bones, back bones, hip bones, rib bones, head bones. Dirty and yellow, bouncing, jumping and twirling, jaunty and jolly, but also chilling, as if our own bones safely inside our own skins might suddenly decide they liked the look of that bone dance and want to join in.

We reached for the bread, but bones like sticks slapped our knuckles and tapped our heads and stabbed at our sides or played our spines like xylophones. It hurt, it stung, it bruised and broke skin. Gap-toothed skulls with eyes full of ants grinned and mocked and chattered as they drove us back, biting at our noses and ears. Under the onslaught we retreated to the gap and the bones all gathered in a dancing mob between us and the bread.

'Now what?' said Sheila. 'If we don't get my bread back everyone's going to get turned into birds!'

'All right then,' I said, and waved at the mass of people crammed into the path, nursing their cuts and bruises, to clear a gap down the middle. When the path was open, I put my fingers to my lips and whistled. Well I tried, nothing happened except for a long flat puff of breath. I'm actually not very good at whistling. Derek gave a sneer, raised his fingers, took a deep breath – but before he could blow, a massive piercing blast tore through the air. Helen lowered her fingers from her mouth looking satisfied.

The pigs of Knockmealldown came galloping down the path.

They were the ghost pigs of Ghost Pig Estate, doomed to haunt the place of their suffering for all eternity. There was absolutely no reason in the world why they should help the people of Knockmealldown. But Mum and Dad and me were blow-ins, outsiders. We had nothing to do with the factory or the pollution or the building of the Estate. We were the only people living in the Estate, the only company they had, the only sign of life in that lonely desolate place. We were vegetarians, too, which might have helped.

They charged into the graveyard, right through the forest of dancing bones, shrugging them aside, trampling them down, crunching them to pieces.

'CHARGE!' I yelled, and we followed them in, grabbing and punching and throwing bones this way and that while the ghost pigs used their snouts to nose the rolls of bread out of their piles and along the mossy broken ground and through the graves. Out of the gap, along the path, across the road, and then rolling down the hill.

Hundreds of hard black bread-rolls bouncing, striking the walls of houses, shattering panes of glass and denting the occasional car. A hundred ghost pigs pushing them along, snorting and squealing in a happy ghost-piggy riot. Thirty crazed, exhausted Knockmealldowners running madly to keep up while hundreds of animated bones beat, bashed, poked and prodded them.

The thunder of the rolls, the squealing and clatter of the pigs, the screaming, roaring, swearing and cursing of the people, the furious clatter, chatter and clacking of the bones would have been enough to wake the dead if the dead weren't already there and having the time of their lives. Or deaths.

The riotous racket must have woken the Good Folk out of their sulk, because they came crowding out of the white mist and the Floating Palace and surged through Ghost Pig Estate to stand at the bottom of the hill. The pure amazement on their Otherworldly faces changed to hilarity and delight as we swept like an avalanche down Main Street and came to a messy stop in a great shuddering, shaking pile at their feet. The loaves rolled down on the Folk. They yelled and caught them and threw them in the air and tossed them back and forth to each other. Pigs and people and bones slid to a sore and weary halt and collapsed en masse. The fight and the flight had gone out of all of us.

I picked up a loaf in each hand and presented them to the King and Queen. I even went down on one knee. The bread was dusty from the chase down the street, but the Good Folk didn't seem picky. The King and Queen accepted them eagerly. They broke the loaves in half and breathed in the scent that rose from inside. Smiles of surpassing ecstasy and joy filled every face. They daintily bit and nibbled the crusts, then chewed the bread, shaking their heads with great slow happy shakes of sheer disbelief that anything in all the worlds in all the universes could possibly taste this good.

The hour was up. Breakfast was served.

'I've a bone to pick with you,' gasped Derek, freeing a struggling rib out of the tangle of his shirt and throwing it over his shoulder.

'Them bones, them bones them dry bones,' sang Helen, and Derek and me roared with laughter. The weary bones all stood up and began hopping back up the street.

'Oh the toe bone's connected to the foot bone, the foot bone's connected to the ankle bone . . .' we sang as they went.

The King and the Queen and the Cluaracan approached, all chewing bread, their mouths and hands stained black, the smell of treacle and turf everywhere. We stopped singing.

'That,' said the King through a mouthful, pausing to swallow. 'That is a story we will be telling for a long time to come. I think we'll call it Brian's Breakfast, and all other breakfasts will be measured by it. That was a fine breakfast, we'll say, but there's none can compare to the breakfast served by Brian Nolan. Oh, our daughter would have laughed at that. You have honoured her this morning, Brian Nolan, by accident or design.'

I glanced at Fester who was sitting by herself, her legs splayed, her wings hanging loose and her beak drooping, her cave-eyes studying the ground between her feet. She was the only one of the Folk not stuffing her face with the Festival Bread of Knockmealldown.

'Was it by accident or was it by design?' asked the Queen, looking suddenly suspicious. 'Did you steal our bread merely to contrive this spectacle? Was this planned?'

'No!' I said. 'I didn't steal the bread! It wasn't me!'

'Brian,' said Bob. 'If that's true, you have to tell us how you knew where the bread was hidden and who put it here.'

'It was— '

'I think it's clear who the guilty party is,' said the Cluaracan, stepping forward. 'This Brian Nolan is a creature of such unparalleled malice that never in all my unborn days have I seen before! I say let justice be swift and brutal as an example to all.'

He raised his stick over his head, a long knobbly blackthorn stick with a lump at the end. Blackthorn sticks aren't walking sticks. They're weapons. Hard as iron, they can cave a person's head in with a single blow.

'NO!' screamed Helen.

'NO!' commanded the Queen.

'Now hold on a minute,' said the King.

But the stick fell. Fester shot in front of me and raised a wing to meet the stick. There was a terrible, ugly crack.

'Ow,' said Fester.

'Fester!' I wailed.

Fester's wounded wing hung from her shoulder like a torn rag. There was no blood, and you couldn't tell by looking at her glowing eyes whether she was hurt or not.

'Sorry,' she said. 'It was an accident.'

'What are you talking about?' I said. 'You saved me!'

'Didn't mean to,' said Fester, looking up at the Cluaracan, almost pleading. 'It was an accident.'

'Your Majesties, I apologise,' the Cluaracan said with a deep, contrite bow. 'Forgive my impulsive act; I was so repelled at the actions of this Brian Nolan monster that I acted without thinking to save the Great Festival from any more of his outrageous tricks.'

'Well,' said the King. 'It's lucky no one was hurt. We'll

save that until the end of the Festival.'

'No one?' I said. 'What about Fester? Her arm!'

'Oh,' said the King, looking vague and puzzled. 'There was someone . . . wasn't there? Who . . .?'

'Please,' said Sheila stepping forward. 'Let's put this behind us.'

'In the name of the baker of the Festival Bread,' said the Queen, crunching on a crust. 'We will put this behind us. Let us return to the Floating Palace. Let the Festival continue.'

'And my mum and dad?' I asked, barely daring to hope.

The King and Queen looked grave and thoughtful.

'We have heard disturbing reports,' said the Queen, glancing at the Cluaracan, who gave a tiny bow.

'There is talk of an enchantment cast on the fiddle,' said the King. 'An enchantment that made all who heard its music dance, cast by a boy.'

'A boy who looked like you,' said the Queen. 'This casts a shadow on your achievement here.'

'We are puzzled and suspicious,' said the King. 'Until we are satisfied that there was no wrong-doing on your part, we will not release your parents.'

I bowed my head, and felt very tired. When I looked up the King and Queen were gone, but I glimpsed the Cluaracan, retreating with the rest of them.

'Hey, you, come back!' I yelled, trotting after him. 'You owe me two pieces of Cloak! And no pesky riddles, you big ugly bullying twerp! Just give 'em to me and get lost!'

The Cluaracan whirled round and waved one hand

airily and arrogantly while he leaned with the other on that rotten stick of his.

I thought I'd hated things before. I thought I hated the way my granny boiled cabbage. I thought I hated earwigs, and that old punk rock music Dad likes so much. I thought I hated Knockmealldown and the Festival. I even thought I hated the flippin' Cluaracan after all he'd done. I'd been upset to the point of tears by the sheer mindlessness of his vandalism: he'd built the factory that polluted the Lake, he'd built the Estate full of Smell, he'd done everything he could to wreck the Festival. But that was all just dislike and distaste and disapproval compared to the burning hot hate at the sight of him, with his cheerful grin and his friendly gestures and his casual pose after HITTING FESTER WITH THAT STICK, which awoke in me now.

'I'm terribly sorry if all this is inconvenient to you,' he said. 'I'll forego the riddle just this once, or we'll be here all day and get nothing done. The pieces of the Cloak are in Una's Salon.'

He waved his stick in the air. 'Go fetch your prize! I've seen more poetry in a slug and more intelligence in a thistle but I'm sure you'll manage to find your way there somehow. Ask for Taffe's Hammer.'

He twirled away, and the Festival Committee closed around me.

'So what you're sayin' is, you did steal the bread?' said Derek. He shook his head. 'Didn't know you had it in you.'

'But I didn't!' I said insistently. 'Look, guys, it's obvious it was the Cluaracan! He charmed the fiddle after charming himself to look like me! Then while everyone was dancing he had the skeletons steal the bread. I don't know if he'd have let us keep dancing till we died or just dropped, but all he wanted was to spoil the breakfast so the Festival would be wrecked completely!'

'I think dancing to death would have spoiled things a bit, too,' said Helen.

'We're not done yet,' I said. 'Listen, I know where the next two pieces are!'

'This is most peculiar,' said Bob, interrupting. He had been listening to our babble with an air of alarm and bewilderment. 'There's stuff going on here that you're not telling me about, isn't there? Come on, out with it!'

'Okay, but . . . but . . .' I said. I looked desperately in the direction of the Salon. It seemed unusually crowded. 'Let's go to Una's first and get the Cloak. It'll only take a sec.'

'Was just thinkin' I needed a perm,' said Derek.

'I'm sorry,' I said, seeing Bob and Sheila's looks of frustration and annoyance. 'Everything's been so hectic and to be honest I haven't really been sure what's going on, but I've a better idea now.'

Before we went to Una's, though, we went back up the street and stopped at the pubs to use the loos. Normally when telling stories you leave bits like that out, but I wanted to mention it because afterwards everyone felt just a little bit better.

3.

TAFFE'S HAMMER

'WE'RE THREE QUARTERS of the way there!' said Fester swaying slightly, holding her limp arm, an odd light turning her cavernous eyes from dark to grey. 'Who'd have believed it? Where did you say the bramble-brained sozzler left it?'

'Una's,' I said. 'Just over there. Coming?'

Instead of answering she swayed back and forth as if about to faint. I turned and stooped down and she fell against my shoulders. Helen helped her sit piggy-back with her good arm around my throat, only slightly choking me.

There was a crowd at Una's door, of Mulligans and Traceys, all ignoring each other and making pointed comments about each other. Helen pushed her way through and we followed. Inside the two entrants for the Long Lisa Contest were being prepared for their ordeal.

'Long Lisa' was the title granted to whoever won the beauty contest usually held on the Sunday night of the Festival. Long Lisa was the bandit queen who used to live in the Tower on the Lake of Lisashee. I wasn't sure if being immortalised in a beauty contest would have impressed her very much, but what did I know? It was tradition.

Mary Mulligan and Catherine Tracey were this year's contestants; they were wearing big lacy gowns, complicated curling hairdos and expertly applied make-up. Una was really good. They looked as if they belonged on a red carpet. But they were also on strike.

'Nope,' said Mary. 'Not doin' it.'

'Do it yourself if you want it done so bad,' said Catherine.

'What's going on?' I said.

Una, carrying a box of the extra-strength hairspray, nodded towards the chairs at the back where four banshees were sitting in a row under the hair dryers, reading magazines, having their nails done and humming along to the Elton John Hour on the local radio station.

'They got chatting with the ladies over there,' said Una. 'And they mentioned that they were entering the competition, and the banshees congratulated them and told them that this year the runner-up would be turned into a bird of paradise with the beautiful plumage in all the colours of a tropical jungle, and the winner would be turned into a white marble statue that would stand at the centre of a Royal maze full of monsters and death traps so that only the most brave and hardy would be worthy to see her. So the girls said no, and they quit.'

'Don't blame 'em,' said Derek. 'I am so done with this flippin' Festival.'

Una took the box of extra-strength hairspray to the banshees, snapping on a face mask and goggles before taking out a can and giving it a shake. Catherine and Mary stuck their heads in magazines and refused to say another word.

'Una,' I said, before she could start spraying perfumed poison everywhere. 'Do you have a hammer here? We were told to ask for a hammer . . .'

Una pulled down her face mask, looking puzzled.

'A hammer?' she said. 'This isn't a hardware shop, Brian. We've no hammers here.'

'Oh the rotten, boil-faced, wart-headed liar!' I said. 'He's done it again!'

Una shrugged helplessly.

'Hang on,' said Derek. 'Did you say a hammer? Wasn't Mick Taffe your uncle, Una?'

'Great uncle, yeah,' she said, and her face cleared as understanding dawned.

'Taffe's Hammer!' said Helen.

'What the heck are you talking about?' I was utterly mystified.

Helen pointed at the wall behind the till where, hanging amongst the black-and-white photographs of movie stars and their hair-styles, was a battered and weathered-looking hurley – a long, flat, wooden stick used to wallop the ball, and sometimes the other players, in a game of hurling. Tied in knots near the top of the handle were two scraps of material. The cloak.

'Mick Taffe,' said Derek in a voice of grave respect. 'The most savage player to ever come out of Knockmealldown. They say he hospitalised more men than World War Two with that thing. They say they offered his hurley to a Museum of Deadly Weapons but they turned it down because there was too much blood on it.'

'Ah, Uncle Mick was a softy,' said Una. 'Off the field. On

the field he'd have clattered his own granny. What do you want with his hurley?'

'We just want the two bits of Cloak tied to the end,' I said, reaching for it. I stood on my tip-toes, stretching, trying not to drop Fester. Una kindly reached past me and got it down for me.

'Now who put them there?' she wondered, trying to undo the knot. 'Weren't there yesterday, that's for sure. Won't come off either.'

We picked at the feathery scraps. They wouldn't budge.

'Sure, take it with you,' Una said. 'You won't want to miss the match, and maybe you can get 'em loose while you watch. Drop it back when you're done, okay?'

She pulled the face mask back up and the goggles down and began spraying the banshees. We fled the billows of gas.

'Shouldn't we try to sort this out?' said Helen. 'I mean, if there's no beauty contest how will we finish the Festival?'

'Heck with that,' I said. 'We'll think of something. We need to find out about the last Feat. I can't believe it. Three Feats down. Only one to go.'

'Let's not count our feathers yet,' said Helen. 'He'll be desperate to stop you now. Can you imagine what'll happen to him if he's found out?'

'I know one thing I'd like to happen to him,' I said grimly, giving Taffe's Hammer a swing. It was too big for me, really, and a bit heavy for a hurley. My hand tingled where I held it and the tingle seem to spread up my arm. In that moment I saw flashes of bodies flying, heard the crack of hurleys clashing and the thunder of boots on grass.

Helen poked me with an elbow. I jumped.

'Come on,' she said. 'Bob and Sheila are going to pitch a fit if we don't tell him what's going on with Fester and the Cluaracan and the Feats soon.'

Bob and Sheila had gathered a crowd on the street, near the entrance to the Estate. Tables and chairs had been brought out and a more human breakfast was being served. Someone had apparently suggested putting on a fry but Bob and Sheila had made a few pointed remarks about the phantom bacon that had just helped save our bacons, and everyone conceded that the vegetarian option was the polite choice, so there was a lot of toast and cereal and fruit being passed around and mugs of tea and coffee.

Out on the Pond, a light haze rose from the water, filled with golden sunlight, not so much hiding the Palace and the Isle as making them fade away. A strange silence fell, broken only by the caws of the invisible crows circling Long Lisa's Tower. Traceys and Mulligans drifted down from Una's looking for some breakfast. Mary and Catherine nibbled toast and sipped tea in their lacy grandeur, sitting on upturned buckets.

I sat down and explained to the crowd what I thought was going on. That the Cluaracan had conspired to have the pig factory and the Estate built next to the lake. The Folk had been furious. Only the intervention of the Princess had saved Knockmealldown from being cursed by the Folk. Nonetheless, without the goodwill of the Folk, Knockmealldown's luck had turned bad, and had turned worse when the Princess had vanished.

I looked at Fester.

Her left wing was hanging loose and crooked at her side but she waved her right wing with a flourish. The humans looked at her and then at me skeptically. Someone gave a bitter laugh. Derek glowered.

'LEAVE IT OUT! Don't mind them, Festy. They don't know enough to know they don't know nothin'.'

'Go ahead, Fester,' said Helen. 'If anyone else makes a peep we'll deal with them.'

I wondered if a creature old enough to have been around for the very first Festival really needed much encouragement from a few human children. Then I remembered how she'd looked at the King and Queen from her deep dark eyes. Time and age worked differently for them. She was always and eternally the young Princess. I felt something thump inside my chest. It's hard for anyone to be kept away from their mum and dad.

She flapped her working wing and swung her beak around and did little jumps on her yellow legs.

'Thank you for your kind mocking laughter!' she said, and went on to tell them what she'd told us earlier about the Cluaracan. He was determined to destroy the Festival and Knockmealldown. Thanks to his efforts, the King and Queen were angry and offended, and had threatened to turn all of the villagers into birds if they weren't happy, and so far the reviews were a bit mixed. When she finished there was a long silence.

'What are we going to do?' someone asked after a few minutes.

'We need to get out of here!' said Tom Tracey. 'We need to get as far away from here as we can! But sure we can't, can we, thanks to that lot!'

He gestured towards Ghost Pig Estate and the Floating Palace beyond in its cloak of mist.

'And miss the rest of the Festival?' said Tricia Mulligan. 'What about the Under 13s hurling match? The beauty contest? If we don't crown someone Long Lisa for the year then we'll have no Long Lisa!'

'She said they'll turn us into birds!' said Tom. 'What good'll having a Long Lisa do us if we're birds? How can the Under 13s win a match if they're all robins or swallows?'

'If we run away we're not worthy of Long Lisa!' declared Tricia. 'And we'll lose the match for the first time in history!'

'Long Lisa wasn't a bird! Birds weren't worthy of Long Lisa!' insisted Tom. 'And we only win the match every year because it's a walkover!'

'Fine! Stay here and be a bird then!' said Tricia, apparently forgetting which side she was arguing.

'Fine, I will!' said Tom, likewise.

They glared at each other in confusion. The group split down the middle and there was muttering and the shaking of heads. Tensions were high; I'd hoped Fester's story would bring everyone together but it had done the opposite. Bob and Sheila were on their feet trying to be calm and reasonable, but everyone was tired and sore and cranky and now scared.

Derek jumped up.

'Well, I'm gettin' ready for the match!' He hopped around, jittery and nervy.

'Do you think the Folk'll play?' I asked, feeling a touch of mild panic at the thought. Calm down, I told myself. A bunch of Folk kids playing a friendly match with a bunch of human kids. What could go wrong?

The feeling of panic got slightly worse.

'Course they will! It'll be epic! We'll give them somethin' to think about, ay? Turn us into birds? We'll turn 'em into losers! Will I see you there, lads? Will you come watch?'

Helen and me looked up. He was talking to us.

'Yeah,' I said. 'Of course. Wouldn't miss it!'

'We'll make flags!' said Helen.

He grinned with delight.

'Up Knockmealldown!' someone shouted. The argument had boiled away like water in a saucepan, leaving everyone embarrassed and self-conscious. Someone sang a few bars of 'Eye of the Tiger'.

'Yeah!' yelled Derek, jumping high and punching the air. 'That's what I'm talkin' about! Lads, lads, I'll be late, come on!' He bounced up and down.

'We'll catch up!' I said, and he was off, while we watched him go.

'You up for the match?' I said to Fester.

'Oh yes, of course!' she said, and abruptly sat down, a dazed, lost look in her dark eyes. 'You'll have to excuse me for a minute or twenty. I'm still not over flying a million miles with you hangin' off me like a half-ton of butter.' Between us we picked her up and tried to set her standing. She felt light and delicate as an eggshell and sagged bonelessly. I had Helen put her on my back again, with her good wing around my neck and her legs around my waist. Her gnarled yellow claws poked out in front of me like the arms of an alien robot. I heard her snore softly into my shoulder blades.

'Shall we be cheerleaders, then?' Helen asked as we followed Derek up Main Street at a slower, wearier pace.

'Okay,' I said, using Taffe's Hammer as a walking stick. 'Just don't try one of those human pyramid things, okay? I'm sore enough from the dancing.'

'Maybe we could deck out Lackley and the auld fella's dog in the colours,' Helen said.

'They can do the pyramid thing.'

'They'd probably be better at it.'

'We can do a Mexican wave. I'll mostly do the sitting part, you can do the standing part. It'll be like a frozen Mexican wave in the Arctic circle.'

'We'll need a chant or two.'

'How about "Go our side! Score more things! Keep sporting! Sport better than the others!" I'm sorry, I'm very tired. Mum is good at chants, you know. She can do great chants. And Dad could make you placards and flags. He could do epic dioramas depicting legendary sporting victories!'

Helen was quiet for a moment.

'They'll be okay,' she said. 'You'll see. They do make lovely herons.'

'They make lovely everythings. Whatever they are, they're lovely. They're the loveliest.'

'Yeah, they are. Come on. We'd better head for the pitch.'

I hoped Fester's wing would be okay. It didn't seem to be hurting her, but what did I know about the magical wings of Otherworld Princesses? Maybe the Good Folk healed quickly? Or had magic healing potions and things? Or was that all Dungeons and Dragons? I wanted to tell her what a Mexican wave was. She'd think it was an actual wave made of Mexicans.

I held the hurley tight, sick with a mixture of excitement and worry. Three down. One to go.

4.

FESTIVAL RULES

WE TURNED LEFT at the Church. A few minutes walk down the road was the hurling pitch, as drab and ramshackle as the rest of Knockmealldown. The walls were grey, the gate was covered in flaking paint and the dressing rooms were falling apart and smelled of bad socks and worse toilets. The pitch, however, was lovingly maintained, and the lines of white paint on the grass were bright and fresh.

I'd had no particular desire to play since we came to Knockmealldown, but Dad still went to matches played during the year, and sometimes I went with him. The only matches were between Under 13s because anyone older usually left Knockmealldown or stopped caring about sport.

Already at the sidelines were the parents of the players, their brothers and sisters and those who could be dragged along. There was a scattering of die-hard supporters who turned up at every match in searing heat or driving arctic rain to yell the lads on.

On the other side were the Other Crowd. They had made a large wooden stand for themselves with comfortable seats and a roof of woven rushes to keep off the sun. It was draped in colourful tapestries and huge rippling pennants and flags. They had drummers and pipers making a racket. It was as if they'd sawn the Roman Coliseum in two and plonked one half down next to the pitch. The Queen was sitting in the place of honour, but I couldn't see the King.

Helen and me, Fester still snoozing on my back, the breath from her beak tickling the hairs on the back of my neck, made our way up to where Derek and the rest of the Under 13s were in a huddle with Bob, who, on top of every other thing he did, was the coach and trainer. His word was law, and those words could be heard clear across six counties in the teeth of a northern gale whenever he thought the right full forward needed to be informed he was failing to properly mark his man with sufficient zeal.

'Never mind them, lads,' Bob was saying. I could see they were shivering despite the heat of the day. They looked pale and wide-eyed, as if they were just a pack of kids. Well, they were a pack of kids. Derek was trying to look fierce and determined. It almost worked. He gave us a nod. We gave him a nod back.

Bob went on. 'Once you're out there with fists full of ash you become men! You become giants! You become warriors who'll fight to the very last, clawing and biting and gouging . . .'

The hurley in my hand seemed to jump, and I nearly dropped it.

'Metaphorically, lads, metaphorically! I'm talking about spirit, not actual clawing and biting and gouging. If I see any of that sort of thing I'll have you out of here so fast you won't have time to change your socks!'

They nodded and looked at him with wide, hopeful eyes, seeking reassurance and certainty and approval from this pillar of strength.

'You'll be grand, lads,' barked Bob. 'Mark your man. Send the ball high. Get in there at the puck-out and keep it movin' fast! Wear 'em down and use your skills! We've worked hard on 'em, so use 'em! Hop the ball and keep passing it forward! Just do your best and you'll have nothing to be ashamed of! Off you go! Go! Go! Go!'

The game of hurling is played with teams of fifteen. Each player is armed with a slender stick of ash called a hurley, and the object of the game is to score goals and points with a small, hard ball called a sliothar. Goals go under the crossbar, points go over it, three points to a goal. It's one of the fastest games in the world, and, at its best, one of the most graceful. High levels of skill and fitness are required to hit and carry the sliothar with the hurley, to tackle and chase and cover the whole pitch for fifty minutes. It is also a tough, bone-crunching game. Bodies collide with bodies, hurleys clash with hurleys, and sometimes, unfortunately, hurleys collide with bodies.

For all that, Derek and the rest of the Under 13s did not expect to risk anything more than a bruised knuckle or a grazed knee. At worst a sprained ankle or an accidental clatter bounced off the helmet. Still, we could tell they were nervous. It looked lonely and cold out there on their spots. They swung their hurleys and bounced up and down and wondered what the hold-up was.

The ground started to tremble and shake. For the first time in a hundred years, the Folk were fielding a team. They came trotting onto the pitch, two-by-two.

'Oh dear,' said Helen. 'They don't look as if they're under thirteen.'

'Six foot under, some of them,' I said.

Four of them were hulking giants. One of the giants was completely made of jagged stone. Their hurleys were as big as church doors. There was a spider thing with a thin body and ten or eleven legs, three skeletons, a floating piece of ragged red fabric about the right size to wrap around a thirteen-year-old boy like a shroud, some angry-looking leprechauns, and the King, who was also captain. They wore kit of blue and red, white shorts and hurling shoes with studs on the bottom. The Queen applauded and all the Good Folk rose to their feet or hooves or claws. Over on the human side there was consternation.

'They can't be expected to play against that lot, can they?' said Helen.

'I think we might need to go for a walkover,' I said. 'Come on.'

'Whazzappenin?' said Fester, into my ear. 'Izza battle started yet?'

'It's not supposed to be a battle,' I said. 'It's just a friendly match.'

I laid Fester gently down on the grass next to the sideline and followed Bob as he ran onto the pitch to confront the oddly familiar referee.

'What the hell do you think you're doing?' he screamed

hoarsely. 'This is supposed to be an Under 13s match! You can't play my lads against that lot!'

'I can tell you most assuredly and without any doubt that every single member of that team is under thirteen hundred,' said the Cluaracan, holding the whistle ready to blow. He was in white shorts and under his brown tweed coat he wore a referee's black jersey. His tweed coat was unbuttoned and every now and then as he swung this way or that I caught a glimpse of the black and silver lining. 'Now perhaps you could leave the pitch and let the game get underway. I have a red card here somewhere, if you don't.'

Bob took off his cap and threw it to the ground, a declaration of war.

'That's unfair!' said Helen. 'Look at them! They'll be slaughtered.'

'You can't be the referee!' I yelled, jabbing Mick Taffe's hurley at him. I felt weird, as if I was going to start fighting with him, which was obviously stupid. 'That's not fair! You're on their side!'

The Cluaracan merely pulled out a red card, waved it in my face and pointed to the sidelines.

'There is no way I'm puttin' my lot up against that shower o' monsters and beasties,' wailed Bob. 'Two of those fellas have three heads! The rules state—'

'My dear sir, perhaps you are unaware, but today's match is to be played according to Festival Rules. It's not my fault if you haven't taken the trouble to familiarise yourself with them and prepared your team accordingly. Now, either get off the field or forfeit the match.'

Bob looked at his boys, shaking with fear most of them, even Derek. They hadn't dropped their hurleys, though. They'd play if he told 'em to. They'd go up against a whole army of monstrosities for his sake. He knew that. It was enough to know that.

'All right, lads,' he said. 'Off you go.'

'What a pity,' said the Cluaracan as they filed off in humiliated relief. 'The crowd will be disappointed. I suppose this is all the fault of the Festival Committee, again. I shall have to tell the King and Queen that you were not properly prepared for the match and we will have to wait another hundred of your years for the next one.'

I stormed over to the King, who was swinging his hurley impatiently.

'He's been lying to you!' I yelled, barely aware of what I was saying, just shouting because it felt good to shout. 'He gave the bikes to the banshees and charmed the fiddle and stole the bread! He's trying to wreck the Festival and blame it on us!'

The King looked down at me with cold, narrowed eyes.

'To accuse one of the Good Folk of interfering with the Festival is to accuse them of the impossible,' he said. 'Grave and terrible spells are laid on us all to protect human and Folk from malice and trickery and violence for these two days. The Cluaracan is a crafty fellow, I grant you, and his exploits have entertained and enraged us since the dawn of time, but not even he, not once in all those thousands of years, has broken the protections of the Great Festival.'

'How would you know?' I shouted, getting a little hysterical. 'He stole your own daughter and turned her into a half-bird thing and paraded her around right in front of you and you never recognised her! Your own daughter, you blind muppet!'

The King's eyes went flat with rage and his lips went thin and pale. His antlers seemed to creak and grow darker and sharper and thornier.

'How dare you,' he whispered.

'Um,' I said. I may have gone just a little too far.

'On the first morning I told you that this Festival must be of a standard that honoured my daughter's memory,' said the King in an icy, detached tone. 'Instead, though not without entertainment, it has been a shambles from start to finish, and now you combine discourtesy with brazen lies and outright insults. Very well. This is your last chance. We wish for a match. A friendly match between humans and Folk. Give us such a match. Win, and we will leave with our blessings. Lose, and we'll make birds of every last one of you.'

'No,' I said. 'I'm sorry, no, don't do that! We can't win! We don't have a team!'

He turned away with a haughty sneer. The Cluaracan came up swinging his whistle around on the end of its chain.

'There's your next Feat for you!' he said to me casually. 'Take up your hurley, play the game and win the match, then the final part of the Cloak will be yours! This should be some Feat, my boy!'

'But I, I . . .'

I can't do it on my own, I was going to say. I don't have anyone to play with. Instead I lifted the hurley and held it in both hands. I stared at the Cluaracan and didn't bother to try and hide that I was tired and scared and weak and not actually very good at hurling. I had everything to lose, but it was time to go down swinging.

'I'll take you on,' I said. 'Let's see what a famous victory you can have against one small boy.'

The Cluaracan snorted and the King rolled his eyes.

'Hey look!' Helen called. 'Look!'

She was pointing towards a group of people who were jogging purposefully onto the pitch. They were carrying hurleys but dressed in everyday clothes. They were led by Tom and Tricia.

'We'll fill in for the lads,' said Tom. 'Be a shame otherwise.'

'Anyone got a coin for the flip?' said Tricia.

'You?' said Bob. '*You* want to play *them*?'

'Well we didn't get all dressed up for nothing, did we?' said Tom.

Tricia grinned.

'Not a day under thirteen hundred,' she said.

'But you can't play them!' Bob gestured despairingly at the Good Folk. 'They'll eat you alive!'

'Oh now, that's silly,' said the Cluaracan. 'They ate before they came out.'

'If they want to eat anything, let 'em try to eat us,' said Tom. 'I'm not getting turned into a thrush without puttin' up a fight!'

'We're the Indigestibles,' said Tricia.

'Right lads, take your marks!' said Tom, rolling up his sleeves.

Traceys and Mulligans, men and women, jogged to their positions.

'You're short a few,' said Bob.

Helen took off her jacket and called for a hurley. Derek ran in off the sidelines carrying two. He handed one to Helen and gave the other a practice swing.

'Guys,' I said.

Bob looked wild with fear and horror. He waved his arms around and stamped up and down a few times before pulling at his hair and picking up his hat.

'You're all mad. Mad! I should be shot for going along with this!' He took off his sweatshirt and threw it at me, then hefted his hurley onto his shoulder and stood beside Derek. 'Let's give 'em heck.'

'Here,' said Sheila, running up and swinging a hurley of her own. 'I'll show them what I think of baking bread for them in their kitchens. I'll show 'em what I think of turning my friends into birds.'

'Oh God,' I said, suddenly feeling a weird mixture of hope and despair. The thing about places like Knockmealldown is that for centuries boys had been given hurleys and sliothars to play with while they were still in the crib, and for the last few decades now, so had most of the girls. I was the weakest player on the field, and yet I was supposed to captain the team and win the match. How was that supposed to work? I forced a fake grin onto my face and some fake cheer into my voice.

'Thanks everyone! Good luck! Don't get hurt! I think we're a man up, so who wants to be sub?'

The Cluaracan was watching me narrowly.

'The rules do allow for a scratch team, I suppose,' he said. 'Still, you don't stand a chance.'

'No?' I said. He was probably right, but who knew? I felt something wild and mad take flight inside me. 'It'll be some Feat if we win, won't it?'

'I suppose it will,' said the Cluaracan with an arch smile.

'Wait a minute,' said the King, interrupting. 'Do you know, we're short a man.'

'You are?' I said, tearing my gaze away from the Cluaracan's intense stare.

'You've plenty to choose from over there,' said Bob.

'We do,' said the King smoothly. 'But it's the custom for one place on our team to be taken by a human. I see you have one too many. Brian you have provided us with the match I requested. Let me reward you. I see you already have the magic hurley of our favourite player. *Mick Taffe come out to play!'*

I felt myself grow. I felt my muscles strengthen. I felt my head fill with knowledge of another person's life. I felt myself change. I was wearing a hurling strip and hurling boots. I was taller and broader and I knew hurling as if I was born to it.

'That's the hurley of Mick Taffe,' said the King, smiling pleasantly. I think he was honestly happy that the match was on after all, and he genuinely thought he was doing me a royal favour. 'One of the greatest hurlers of the century. Many's the time we carried him off to play on our matches, but he's long gone now. His spirit will help you play, Brian, and you will help us win.'

I tried to object, but the ghost of Mick Taffe had possessed me completely. Mick Taffe made me take a swing of the hurley and jog to our position on the side of the Good Folk. He made me hawk and spit (disgusting!), then crouch down ready for the off. The giants and the leprechauns and the skeletons and the red cloth thing and the King all took their spots. The spider-thing was their goalie, and it was already spinning a web across the goal mouth. On the other side of the halfway line my friends took their positions.

This was wrong. I was playing with the wrong team. I was supposed to be playing with the humans, not the Good Folk! How could I perform the Feat if I was on the wrong team?

I saw Helen mouth 'What are you doing?' at me and Derek scowl and Bob frown, but I could say or do nothing except glare back with the concentration of a man about to leather the living daylights out of his opponents.

Bob and the King stood side-by-side, ready for the throw-in. Then the Cluaracan blew his whistle, and threw the ball straight to the King.

5.

CLASH OF THE ASH

IN MY MIND I wasn't playing at all. The ghost of Mick Taffe was. In my mind the Challenge was for my team – the human team – to win.

K'lldown 0-0 Good Folk 0-0

The King caught the ball, tossed it, swung the hurley and with a mighty crack sent the sliothar soaring over the other half. The Folk team roared and began to stampede in the general direction of the Knockmealldowners. I sprinted forwards, chasing the ball. Helen leaped and caught the ball, tossed it onto the flat of her hurley, and, balancing it there, ran straight at the oncoming horde. The game was on. Knockmealldown versus the Other Folk, and me. It shouldn't have lasted a minute.

The giants thundered down on the Downers', churning up the turf of the pitch in great gouts of grass and dirt as they went.

I barged into Helen, knocking her sideways. I tried to apologise, but I couldn't. Trapped in my own head, I yelled at Mick Taffe to cut it out, to stop being so rough with my friends. He ignored me as if I wasn't there. The man was a nasty bully, and he was using me to be a nasty bully to my friends, and I hated it.

The ball flew and Derek snatched it out of the air. I was off, straight after him. Mick Taffe knew how to play hurling, and he played it like a demon. I was just a passenger in my own body now. I growled with frustration.

A three-headed giant swung a hurley that was more like the wing of an airplane at Derek. He ducked, dodged, swept round the giant and passed the sliothar up the field, where it found Sheila, who popped it high. An ogre leaped for it, but it shot through his huge fingers, and then through the high bars of the goal.

A flag went up. We all turned to look at the Cluaracan, who pretended to only just notice that all this had been happening while he'd been tying his shoes, and reluctantly blew the whistle. First point to Knockmealldown. The supporters went wild. The Folk crowed out good-natured jeers. Which is to say that a load of crows suddenly erupted out of their midst and flew around the pitch cawing and croaking jibes at both sides.

K'lldown 0-1 Good Folk 0-0

Maybe this wasn't going to be a massacre after all.

Mick Taffe – me – shook his head and spat. It was really disgusting, seriously. The King glanced over at him and gave a nod.

One of the skeletons did the puck-out and the ball flew down the home half and three 'Downers and two leprechauns and the red rag leaped to catch it.

Helen cleared the ball with a leprechaun hanging off her back. I could hear the yelling from the sidelines.

'Go on, lads, go on, go on! Oh God look out!'

Bob was hopping the ball from hurley to hand as he ran, searching for an opening. I hacked at his legs with the hurley and he went crashing to the ground. (NO! I howled inside.) The spider-thing swarmed all over him and began wrapping him in a thick sticky web. Even the Cluaracan had to allow that this might constitute a foul, and he blew.

The spider ignored him and began dragging Bob off the field. Derek and Helen and the 'Downers surrounded it and began battering it mercilessly with their hurleys and pulling at Bob to get him free. Spectators joined in, yelling and berating both the spider thing and the referee, who was starting to look harried and confused. Some of them were shouting at me, but it all seemed far off and muffled, and Mick Taffe didn't care. Mick Taffe was a hard man and a hit-man.

The giants and ogres and skeletons and leprechauns ran to their team-mates' defence, leaving the red rag fluttering gently a foot above the pitch, even though there was no breeze. The King got into the middle of it all and started to smack the spider-thing until it let Bob go. He sent his team back to their goal to cool down and one of the Folk supporters cut Bob free with a pair of golden scissors.

Helen and Derek pulled the cloven web cocoon apart and pried Bob out of its sticky maw. He coughed and hacked and spat something horrible into the torn-up ground. He looked over at me, and Mick Taffe looked stonily back at him. He tested his footing, limped a little. There was a long red bruise on his thigh.

The spectators were heading back to the lines and the Cluaracan was taking the spider's name, and had so far filled three pages with hisses and chitters and burps.

'Right,' said Bob. 'My ball?'

'Your ball,' confirmed the Cluaracan reluctantly. He gave up on getting the spider's full name and threw the notebook and pencil at it and chased it away. The players arranged themselves for the free. The Cluaracan sneered at Bob and whistled at him to take the shot.

Crack. The crowd roared. Point.

K'lldown 0-2 Good Folk 0-0

Fists punched the air. The crowd opened their mouths.

'KNOCK 'EM ALL DOWN KNOCKMEALLDOWN!'

That was it. That was Mum's chant.

'KNOCK 'EM ALL DOWN! KNOCK 'EM ALL DOWN!'

I felt a tickle in my stomach. I felt the beating of my heart. I was no ghost. Mick Taffe was the ghost. I pushed. The weight was incredible. He was so heavy. He was as dumb as a plank and dull as a wet Sunday, but when it came to hurling his will was pure force. I pushed and I pushed.

'KNOCKMEALLDOWN!'

The Folk had the puck-out.

It soon turned out that giants and ogres are not as big an asset on the hurling field as they might at first appear. So long as the opposing players are nimble enough to dodge round their enormous feet and swinging arms and unfairly gigantic hurleys, they're not good for anything other than churning the pitch into a muddy no-man's-land and getting in each other's way.

The three-headed giant got into a loud argument with itself over tactics. The sliothar was too small for the ogres and giants to catch or hold, and the only way they succeeded in pucking it with their hurleys was either straight up or straight down, and play had to come to a complete stop waiting for it to fall back down or get dug back up. There was so much mockery and scorn poured at them from both sets of supporters that they stopped even trying and just huddled together in a miserable group by a corner flag comforting each other and trying not to cry.

But the rest of the Folk were no slouches. The spider didn't try to eat anyone else, but back in goal the web it was spinning was getting thicker and deeper, making scoring difficult. It shot out threads of webbing to catch the ball whenever it was in danger of going over the bar. Knockmealldown appealed to the ref, who shrugged and allowed it.

K'lldown 0-2 Good Folk 0-2

Tom and Tricia accidentally barrelled right into the spider and crashed through the web. When the three were disentangled, the web was wrecked and the spider's web-shooter was blocked by a small stone that had been jammed in so hard it couldn't be dislodged.

The skeletons were tricky as they had a tendency to fall apart and all their bones would go flying to different parts of the pitch, sometimes with the sliothar lodged in a ribcage or an eye socket. Sometimes they would combine, and all their arm bones would fly together, allowing one of them to extend one arm half the width of the pitch, or their back bones, meaning there was a skeleton taller than four people running with the ball, which couldn't be reached by the 'Downers.

The skeletons weren't very sturdy, however, and a little aggressive play, a little bit of colliding and bumping would see them scattered across the pitch, frantically trying to put themselves back together.

K'lldown 0-5 Good Folk 0-6

The leprechauns were fierce players altogether. They knew the form, all right, short as they were. They kept the ball low, skimming it around the torn-up chunks of grass and earth. They played fast, passing it back and forth as they made chances and took open spaces and left their 'Downer markers facing the wrong way or slapping into each other. The 'Downers worked to keep the sliothar off them with lots of high balls. Also, you could just jump right over them, though you had to watch out because they were dirty players and before you knew there'd be four of the little gombeens hangin' off you.

K'lldown 0-8 Good Folk 0-10

Everyone just avoided the flapping red rag, which was mysterious and sinister and seemed to be off in a whole other world of its own, watching and waiting for something, nobody wanted to know what.

Mick Taffe was everywhere, though. The King and me dominated the field. We were deadly, and anyone who came near me got the worst of it, a full body slam, an elbow in the ribs, a clatter across the legs. I flattened Derek and fell heavily on top of him. (LEAVE HIM ALONE, I wailed.)

Helen came charging up and dragged me off and bunched my shirt in her fist.

'Play the ball not the man!' she screamed. 'What's wrong with you, Brian?'

'Traitor!' croaked Derek.

It wasn't Brian looking back at them. But I was getting there. Inside I was scraping away at Mick Taffe's hold. I was slowing him down, making him stumble and miss and trip. He wasn't very bright, so he had no idea what was going on. But I wasn't there yet.

The King and Mick passed the ball between them, bounding about the pitch with leaps, sprinting from one place to another, making spaces, catching, hitting. They scored points and goals, and I could only make a few go wide.

K'lldown 2-12 Good Folk 2-13

But somehow the score was level the whole way through, every point and every goal fought for with blood and sweat and tears. As the final minutes approached, the tension was palpable. The shouts were getting fraught and frantic. The players were muttering out loud.

In the last minutes, with the Folk ahead by a point, Bob broke away, hopping the ball, skeletons and leprechauns and the King right on his heels, the giants too timid now to get involved, the spider wrong-footed. He gave the ball a mighty whack and it flew straight and true to the upper left-hand corner of the goal.

K'lldown 3-12 Good Folk 2-13

The whistle blew. Knockmealldown was ahead. Only a few minutes left.

A skeleton took the puck-out. It soared high. Mick Taffe watched it like a hawk, moving to position himself. I pulled and pushed and kicked at him for all I was worth.

The King caught it and ran for the goal. Derek and Helen sprang for him, but he was too fast. Mick Taffe entered the square and bumped the goalie aside, and the King sent the ball rocketing at the net.

I felt the sting in my hand as I caught the ball just before it crossed the line.

Wherever he was, somewhere far, far away Mick Taffe was looking around in confusion and wondering what had just happened. But he wasn't here any more. I hopped the ball onto the hurley and ran like hell for the other goal. Nobody tried to stop me. Nobody knew what was going on. The goal was wide open. I whacked the ball, and it flew straight and true for the back of the net.

From out of nowhere the red rag flung itself in the way, and the ball flew into the rippling red curtain. It fluttered and vanished, ball and all. I looked around, bewildered and saw it reappear way down at the other goal. The ball shot out of its red folds, and the last goal was scored, putting the Folk ahead.

K'lldown 3-12 Good Folk 3-13

The Cluaracan blew. The game was over. The Folk victorious. I wanted to throw down the hurley, but remembered the parts of the cloak still attached to it. The Cluaracan laughed and twirled the whistle on its cord, and the lining of his jacket rippled, full of feathers. I bowed my head and closed my eyes. I had lost. I could have appealed to the referee that there had been cheating and unfairness and foul play, but the referee was the Cluaracan. I didn't think I'd get a fair hearing.

The Good Folk supporters exploded. They whooped and hollered and sang. Fireworks detonated overhead. White doves and black crows and multicoloured parrots flocked and flew and fought and squawked the names of the winning team as if it were a roster of legendary heroes.

The human supporters were silent. Nobody moved.

The 'Downers slumped, weak and tired and limping, feeble and hurting, their minds wandering, their eyes vague, gathered together, holding each other up, slapping each other's backs, leaning on their hurleys, faces sheened and grey with sweat, hair lank and limp. Helen and Derek looked shattered. Sheila dropped her hurley to the ground and stood with her hands on her hips, shaking her head. The spider crept up beside her and started to eat the hurley.

I sat in a hollow gouged out of the ground by one of the giants and swore. Mick Taffe's ghost was gone. Bob stepped towards the King, his hand outstretched. The King looked at Bob, then down at his hand, then turned his back and walked off the pitch. If we'd hoped winning the match might have made him feel more benevolent towards us, we were sorely disappointed. Too much had gone wrong already, and I don't think he'd ever forgive me, or the village, for what I'd said to him about his daughter.

The Folk roared and shouted and celebrated. The 'Downers limped away in silence. I'd failed the Feat. I'd failed the Challenge. The Cloak was lost. Knockmealldown was doomed. It was a miracle we weren't birds already. I groaned and stood up and went to face them and explain why it was I'd helped them lose.

6.

APRÈS MATCH

THREE PIECES OF the Cloak weren't enough to break the charm, Fester regretfully informed me, her long yellow beak drooping sadly. It had been an heroic effort and she was as filled with gratitude as the sun is filled of fire, but it wasn't enough.

I told my friends I'd been possessed by a haunted hurley, and that was why I'd played against them, and hurt them, and bruised them, and scored goals and points against them and lost any chance of getting the rest of the Cloak off the Cluaracan. They believed me.

'It was my own fault,' I said. 'Flippin' Mick Taffe got the better of me. I told the King right to his face what I thought of him. Told him what a fool he'd been. Sorry, Fester.'

'You should have heard what I used to call him after that wart-faced Cluaracan put the spell on me,' she said, dipping her beak into a glass of orange and blowing a stream of sticky fizzy bubbles. Her wing was stiff, but she was using it a little, at least. Everyone was stiff and sore, though. 'It was as if all he could hear were doors blowing closed in far-off rooms. Then he'd fall asleep, the thunderin' eejit.'

'I thought you were tryin' to get back at me,' said Derek. He looked completely miserable. We were all a bit like that. I'd never seen Helen look so down. We were sitting at a table outside Mulligan's and Tracey's. Someone had brought us some drinks and sandwiches and a big jug of water. The 'Downers and their supporters were inside Mulligans. The Other Folk were all inside Tracey's.

The Traceys were livid. They'd refused to serve the Folk and the family and their regular clientele had moved next door, letting the Good Folk have the run of the place. I wasn't sure how they'd gotten the giants in, but we could hear the skeletons' clacking with laughter as they toasted the red rag over and over again.

In Mulligan's there was a lot of drinking, a lot of talking, but not much cheer. People were giving us a wide berth, and everyone was glaring at me darkly. I was an obnoxious, incompetent flippin' traitor, after all.

But my friends believed me. Before all of this had started, two of them had been a pair of pains I couldn't wait to get away from and the other one looked as if she was a runaway from the sort of freak show you only see in old black-and-white horror films. Now they were my friends and they believed me. How about that?

'Get back at you?' I said. We were speaking very slowly with lots of heavy pauses between sentences. We were very, very tired.

'For wreckin' your bike the way I did,' Derek said. 'I'm

sorry. You wouldn't, would you? I would. I'm awful.'

'No,' said Helen. She was halfheartedly trying to untie the pieces of the Cloak from Mick Taffe's Hammer.

'No,' I said.

'I am,' Derek said. 'I would've. I would've done it to get back at you. I would've done it just to torment and blackguard you. For the laugh. You wouldn't. Flippin' boy scout.'

'To be honest, Brian, what worried me was that they'd offered you a deal,' Helen said. 'To save your parents.'

'Nope,' I said. 'Haunted hurley. Between the two of you, though, you're making me feel lucky it was just a haunted hurley. I might have sold my soul or something. Like Long Lisa. Or maybe I did.' I looked around anxiously, feeling sick in my stomach. 'We're on borrowed time now, guys. They're going to turn us all into birds, except for me. The Cluaracan'll want his pound of phantom flesh. Have you seen him?'

I shuddered at the thought. Maybe the best I could hope for was that he'd turn me into a little heron and I could live on the shores of the Pond with Mum and Dad eating frogs and minnows. It might be a happy life. Herons didn't have to run festivals. I didn't think so, though. I was pretty sure that it was a career of phantomhood and moaning in the wilderness for me.

'Nope,' Helen said.

'Come on,' I said, and forced myself upright. Anxiety and dread burned in me like industrial-strength indigestion. I watched every passing figure, human or Folk. I peered into every corner. Where was the Cluaracan? When was he going to turn me into a ghost or whatever? What could I do?

All the Folk and all the humans seemed to be in the village, so I led the gang through the Estate to the Green, feeling as if I was putting it between me and the Cluaracan.

The long sun of the evening filled the mist on the Pond with a soft rosy light. It looked enchanting. It was, in fact, enchanted. Lackley was lying on the grass with her legs folded under her, serene and calm and beautiful. We sat nearby in a little circle, leaning into each other as we spoke.

'Guys,' I said, panic making my voice high-pitched and cracked. 'We're in so much trouble. Does anyone have any ideas?'

'Get meself fitted for a heron suit,' said Derek.

Fester was doing one-winged cartwheels on the grass. Poor Fester. I wondered if she had always been like this or if her captivity had driven her dotty. She could be quite sensible at times, but it took a lot of effort.

'There really is no way out, is there?' said Helen. 'The King and the Queen hate us and the stupid beauty contest's been abandoned, so the Festival is over. We lost the match. We're doomed.'

Derek gave a long, low groan.

'Hello children,' said Lackley. 'Are you enjoying the Festival?'

We hesitated.

'No,' said Derek. 'It's bloody awful.'

'It's not going very smoothly,' said Helen 'Relations are a bit strained.'

'They turned Mum and Dad into herons,' I said bitterly, and felt a stab of pain go through me. 'And now they're going to turn everyone else into birds too.'

'There have been better Festivals,' said Lackley.

'Really?' I said. 'Which of them were better?'

'All of them,' said Lackley with a sigh. 'I don't really understand it. How did it all go wrong? You really shouldn't have let them dig up the field and put in that pig factory. That was a catastrophic thing to do. I couldn't believe it the year I came out of the Isle to find it there – that horrible, nightmarish place. I nearly stopped coming to the Festival, you know, and stayed in my high green pastures in the Otherworld – but the people here were so miserable I couldn't bear to abandon them. I hoped the Great Festival itself would mend things, but that seems unlikely, what with . . . what with . . .'

'Yes?' said Helen. 'What with what?'

Lackley blinked, a long, slow, gorgeous blink.

'I'm sorry, my dear. Was I saying something?'

'What about the Princess?' I said.

'Princess?'

'The missing Princess! The one they're all broken up over. She's not missing at all, she's right there! It was the Cluaracan who did it!'

Lackley looked away from us, and then back.

'Oh look,' she said. 'They're coming!'

And they were. Giants were vaulting houses and lithe furry creatures with teeth and claws were galloping swiftly and strange wisps of coloured light were zipping through the air on buzzing wings. We moved closer together, back to back and shoulder to shoulder as the giants quaked the ground and surrounded us and the furry creatures prowled around us in a circle, purring, and the wisps hovered over us, darting here and there.

'I told you he would try to escape!' said the Cluaracan, pushing through legs like tree-trunks. 'There they are!'

'I'm not trying to escape!' I replied indignantly, though my stomach was shrinking to the size of a pea.

The giants and fox-things parted for the King and the Queen, and all the short, tall and middling people of the Good Folk milled around us, and behind them came the Knockmealldowners at a run, calling to us, trying to get through the pack.

'This Festival is over,' said the King. 'Though it barely deserves the name.'

'What about the beauty contest?' I said weakly.

'There is no beauty left here,' said the Queen sadly. 'And no great contests either. All joy and sport have fled this place, ploughed under the poisoned soil by the cold steel blades of your foolishness and greed.'

'It's worse you deserve,' said the King. 'But in memory of my daughter and her fondness for you, we shall permit you to live your days in the sky and the trees and the hedges with a song in your heart. I gave you a last chance and you lost. So be it.'

'Oh Daddy, Mammy, you great big eejits,' said Fester. 'Don't do it, please don't do it!'

'All birds, save this one!' said the Cluaracan, pointing at me with his blackthorn stick. 'This one owes me a forfeit! Four Feats he promised me, and he barely scraped the gumption together to manage three, though I took it easy on him!'

'Feats?' said the King, puzzled. 'There was a Challenge, then? Why were we not told? Why was it not part of the Festival? What was the Challenge?'

'Nothing worth bothering with, Your Majesties,' said the Cluaracan hastily. 'Never has there been a Challenge so insipid and embarrassing. Had you been aware of it you would have ended the Festival before it even began to spare yourselves the sorry spectacle!'

'We had to win the match for the final Feat,' I said, dully. 'But the referee here made sure that didn't happen.'

'They lost the match and lost it completely! I hate to do it, Your Majesties, but the laws of the game are written in the burning hearts of the stars! I will be a good master, though he's sure to be a lazy and faithless servant and when he fades to a gibbering shade in some cold damp corner of the Otherworld it'll come as a relief to all of us!'

'No!' I said. 'Wait!'

'It grieves us,' said the Queen. 'Of them all you were the one with spirit and heart and courage. You insulted us and assaulted us, but you rode with the banshees, you danced with the bones, you served us our bread and you played with the giants. You almost reminded us of the times when the Festival of Knockmealldown was truly Great.'

'Then don't do this, Your Majesties!' said Helen. 'Don't let this happen to him! To us! It's not fair! It's the Cluaracan who made everything go wrong! That's your daughter right there! Fester! Oh, why can't you see her?'

'I swear by all that's good and holy,' said Derek. 'If you

turn me into any sort of a flippin' bird I'll fly from one end of the earth to the other to find you and when I do I'll drop a little message on your head, and I'll drop the same message on your head every day for the rest of forever!'

'Let it be done,' said the King. 'Let Knockmealldown be no more, and let us return to the Otherworld, and let there be silence here forever, and that will not be long enough to grieve for our loss.'

A strange noise came from behind the crowd of Folk. All the people of Knockmealldown had been shouting and calling and protesting. Now their voices changed to tweets and shrills and caws and croaks and when they moved it was with a fluttering of feathers.

'NO!' I screamed. I looked at Derek and Helen, their faces sharpening, darting, their eyes black, blinking, their bodies shrinking. The Cluaracan's hand fell heavily on my shoulder.

'You're mine now, me lad,' he said.

'Excuse me,' said Lackley.

The people of Knockmealldown rose in a flock with the sound of a thousand raindrops hammering on leaves.

The Queen bowed her head at Lackley.

'Great lady of the fields,' she said. 'What would you like to say?'

'Oh, it's probably nothing,' she said, slow and ruminative. 'It's just I thought I heard someone say that young Brian here had failed in his final Feat. Did I hear correctly?'

I was on my knees at this point. I didn't care. Fester had a wing around me and the Cluaracan's hand had a tight, biting grip on me. I barely felt the pain, but I could feel his glee thrumming through his fingers. Maybe this would be better, I thought. I'd never have to grow up and fall in love and have a family and get a job. I was going into myth and legend, to become a phantom to scare small children. All my family and all my friends were now birds, and it was my fault. It would be for the best.

'That's right,' crowed the Cluaracan, putting some of the crows milling in confusion above us to shame. 'An abject failure, that's what it was! A humiliating defeat! Oh, I hadn't realised how much fun this would be!'

'I'm confused,' said Lackley. 'I was under the impression that Brian had been playing for the winning team.'

I felt the Cluaracan's hand jerk, and Fester stiffen. I heard a silence fall amongst the Folk. The people kept flying because they were birds and had lost all interest in human things.

'No,' said the Cluaracan. 'It was . . .'

It was the human team that had to win, with me on it. Or was it? Hang on.

Take up your hurley, play the game and win the match, he'd said.

He hadn't said which team had to win!

'She has a point,' said the King, grudgingly. His eyebrows shot up in appreciation. 'Is it possible? I do believe the boy has outsmarted you, Cluaracan.'

'The terms of the Challenge were clear,' said the Cluaracan.

'No they weren't,' I said. 'You didn't say which team! I thought you did, but you didn't!'

'Outsmarted himself,' muttered Fester.

'Oh, brilliantly done!' said the Queen. 'Well played, young Brian! Well played!'

'Yeah,' I said. 'I really showed him, didn't I?'

'Your Majesties,' said the Cluaracan. 'He didn't, that is to say, I meant . . .'

'Sloppy,' said Fester. 'You got careless, you hairy brindlesnout.'

'Oh she would have liked that,' said the King. 'She would have loved that!'

'You're not wrong,' said Fester, clapping me on the shoulder. The Cluaracan still hadn't let go of the other and he pressed down to keep me on my knees.

'Your Majesties!' he protested. 'It was no doing of his! It was I who tricked him! His team lost!'

'The human team lost, yes! But Brian was playing for the team that won!' said the King. 'The boy outplayed whatever game you were playing too, Cluaracan! Why else would he have shown up with Mick Taffe's Hammer in his hand? Brian tricked us fair and square!'

I almost said that I wasn't trying to trick anyone; if anyone was trying to trick them it was the Cluaracan. I'd almost ended up tricking myself. In my exhaustion and fear I'd assumed all along that the *human* team winning had to be the Feat. 'My' team had always been the team with my friends on it. I'd been playing for the 'other' team. And I didn't think it would count because it had been Mick Taffe playing, really, not me. The Folk saw it differently. These were Festival Rules.

I bit my tongue though and, weak with relief, looked over at Lackley, mouthing the words 'Thank you' at her. She gave me a slow, languorous wink and turned away to find some more grass to chew.

7.

HËLHOUSE ON YOUR TAIL

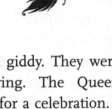

MY TREMENDOUS FEAT had made the Folk giddy. They were dancing and chattering and cheering. The Queen ordered everyone back to Main Street for a celebration. I wanted them to turn everyone back to people again. The Cluaracan's fingers dug cruelly into my shoulder and I cried out with pain. He released me abruptly and without a backward glance strode off with the Folk. Fester helped me up.

'WAIT!' I called, but none of the Folk were listening. I staggered after them. 'WAIT! What about them? What about the birds? Mum and Dad! Helen! Derek! Bob! Sheila! Change them back! Change them back, please!'

The King and Queen must have heard me because they paused and turned back to me, and all the Folk watched as I ran up. We were right in the heart of Ghost Pig Estate. There was our house and there was the pit. The covering of Hëlweed that had been torn off by the banshees had almost completely regrown. The Smell suddenly seemed to thicken around me and made me gag. A strange silence fell, all the birdsong from the panicking Knockmealldowners filling the sky above suddenly cut off. Dwarfed by the houses with their empty window sockets full of yellow weeds and red flowers, the Folk looked ill and uneasy. Even the giants seemed to shrink, the flying wisps to shrivel, the fox-things to whimper.

'Please,' I said, trying not to throw up. 'Please change them back.'

The Queen cleared her throat. Her delicate shade of green had changed to a colour that was downright sickly.

'Perhaps we could talk about this somewhere else,' she said, her voice tight, as if she were trying to speak without taking a breath.

'Brian,' said Fester, tugging at my sleeve. 'Brian, for all love, she's right. Not here! There's something very wrong here! Something awful!'

But to my mind it might as well be here as anywhere else. Why not? I'd had to live in this stinking ruin for the last three years. They were only passing through, like a bunch of tourists. Did they think I liked it? Did they think it was fun? And then they came here and looked down their noses at us and told us we were awful, and threatened us and punished us when one of their own was as much to blame as any human? This was HIS work, and if they were returning to the Otherworld with him they were going to have to get used to it.

'Change them back!' I insisted, a little breathless because it was hard to breathe. 'Before you take another step, change them back!'

The King looked at the Cluaracan, who rolled his eyes

and swung his stick impatiently at a pebble lying on the road.

'Is that your wish?' said the Queen, her voice a little hoarse. 'To have them changed back? What a pity. We cannot do that, unless it was the prize you agreed on. Isn't there something else you would prefer to have? Something you would claim from the Cluaracan? What were the terms of your Challenge?'

'And why *are* we only hearing abut it now?' said the King, coughing a little. 'A Challenge should be made before all, in public, so that it may be applauded and judged and rendered into story and song. It certainly might have livened up this shambles of a Festival.'

'A Challenge from an intemperate child?' said the Cluaracan casually. 'I saw no need to waste your time with such an embarrassment. Where's the sport in the humiliation of one so worthless?'

'And yet it seems he has bested you four times now,' said the Queen. 'Not so worthless, and the humiliation is surely yours. What is his prize? Perhaps he would prefer it to the temporary return of friends and family?'

'Oh a trifle, a bauble, a scrap of nothing,' said the Cluaracan. 'You know what these children are like. Once they set their minds on something, however useless and insignificant, they cannot be deterred by rhyme or reason.'

'Well, so, tell us what it is before we expire of this foul pollution!' snapped the King.

'Very well,' said the Cluaracan. 'Let me tell you where you will find it Brian, then you may show it to their majesties at their leisure. Go, now, beyond water and stone to the hidden—'

'NO!' I screeched like, well, like a banshee. 'Give it to me! Now! Here and now! No riddle, no hiding! Hand it over, now!'

Even the Cluaracan seemed taken aback by my outburst. There was a heavy thump, and the ground shook. One of the giants had fainted from the Smell. Or from the tension. Or both. A leprechaun climbed onto his chest, grabbed a wisp from the air and started to fan his face.

'In the name of the sweet smell of summer blossom give him his scrap before we expire in this privy!' ordered the King.

The Cluaracan's face seemed to shrivel and shrink like a prune, as if he was swallowing something exceptionally sour. A thousand years unfolded in a thickening of wrinkles and lines across his cheeks, brows and eyes.

'Your Majesty,' he said, biting the words like chunks of hardened toffee. He threw open his coat and I saw again the lining of silky silver and black, and a square of cloth flew at me, whirling around and around. I snatched it out of the air. It felt soft and smooth. Fumbling clumsily, I tugged at the scraps tied around the hurley. They finally came free, and unfolded like liquid smoke. I dropped the hurley and held the three quarters of Fester's Cloak of Feathers up for the King and the Queen and all the Folk to see. I was too desperate and impatient and my hands were too full to pull the fourth piece out of my pocket.

'Don't you know it?' I called to them, hoarsely,

desperately. 'Don't you know it when you see it? You loved her so much, can't you see that this was hers? Your Princess! Her Cloak! Her Cloak of Feathers! Look at it! You know it! Please, you must see it! You *have* to see it! It's hers!'

The heads of the Folk turned and the eyes of Folk studied the scraps held up in my hands. Even the head of the fallen giant raised itself a little to have a peek.

'Begad,' said the leprechaun. 'He's right. It's hers.'

'He is,' said the giant. 'I'd know that anywhere, even in pieces like that. Who would tear a thing like that asunder? Who would dare?'

'How did he get it? How he did he come to have such a thing?'

'He won it, through Challenge and Feats, he won it. From . . .'

'From . . .'

And all eyes turned away from me and from the Cloak.

'Cluaracan,' said the King. 'What does this mean?'

'Cluaracan,' said the Queen. 'What have you done?'

The Cluaracan, his face saggy with age and resentment, shook his head slowly, and looked at me.

'I was so close,' he said. 'All I wanted to do was end this Festival once and for all, and wipe Knockmealldown from the map. Then we'd never need set foot outside of the Otherworld for the rest of time, and in all that timeless time she would surely have come to see the error of her ways and come to see that she loved me after all, every bit as much as I love her. Then grieving would have ended and all would be restored.'

'Cluaracan!' said the King. 'Where is our daughter WHERE IS SHE?'

'Quiet, fool,' said the Cluaracan. 'This child has brought your end upon you.'

'She's here!' I held up one of Fester's wings. She waved madly with the other and danced on her yellow feet. 'She's right here!'

The King and the Queen and all the Folk narrowed their eyes and peered at the little figure beside me. With the Cloak no longer in the Cluaracan's possession, his spell of concealment that kept Fester hidden from their eyes was fading. Every single eye went suddenly wide as they finally, finally SAW her. A strange shivering roar of shock and outrage and delight ran through the Folk. It was more like a choir tuning up to sing some epic, intricate harmony where all the different singers had different emotions to express all at the same time.

I thought that was it. I thought we'd done it. In that moment I thought we'd won, and that everything was going to be okay. Everyone would be changed back.

'Brian Nolan you are a pest and a fool and the most poisonous scrap of nettle growing from the top of this hill of dung,' the Cluaracan said. Maybe I was imagining it, but I thought there was a note of admiration in there somewhere. I was probably imagining it. 'It's an awful pity, but none of you will leave this place alive except one, and she will be going with me.'

'CLUARACAN!' roared the King.

'Oh, no!' said Fester. 'Give me the Cloak, Brian, quick!'

I was knocked aside by a ringing blow on my shoulder

om the Cluaracan's blackthorn stick. I cried out as I felt the three pieces of the Cloak snatched from my hand.

'I never said anything about letting you keep them,' I heard the Cluaracan say.

'CLUARACAN!' roared the Queen.

'Stop roaring at him and stop him!' I roared.

Giving one more mighty roar, the crowd of Folk surged forward, giants loping, wisps buzzing, fox-things flowing, leprechauns running and the King and Queen transported to their savage state of talons and teeth and antlers like weapons. Before they could reach us, vines of Hëlweed slithered from the pit on the road, tangling them up and tripping them over.

'You can't just take his lawful prize back like that!' I heard Fester say. 'It's against the rules of a Challenge!'

'I don't care,' said the Cluaracan. 'Now, Princess. Be tall and fast and strong to carry me out of this foul world.'

Fester changed. Flowing and growing, snorting and shaking, from the scrap of feathers and cloth to a small black pony with glowing red eyes, ferocious and strong, almost savage.

The King and the Queen, slashing ferociously at the Hëlweed with their claws, wailed in anger and despair.

The Cluaracan whistled and Fester the pony shot across the road in a clatter of hooves and pebbles and a terrible scream. She turned in a shower of red clay and the Cluaracan sprang onto her back and she was galloping back towards me. Her eyes were blazing, and I almost didn't see the Cluaracan's blackthorn stick as it swung for my head.

I dived for the ground and they went past in a churn o̅ hooves and a mist of flying clay. The Cluaracan laughed and Fester screamed. The ground started to shake and crack and break. All around us the ghost houses were shivering and crumbling, and great masses of yellow shoots and red flowers came boiling out of windows and doors.

The houses rose out of their foundations on moving columns of Hëlweed that walked towards the Folk. Limbs made of twisted layers of Hëlweed reached for the Folk through gable walls like arms. Great masses of Hëlweed surfaced through rooftops. Slates, timber and scraps of insulation sloughing off like old skin. The Hëlweed wore the houses like armour as they surrounded us, cutting us off from the lake and the fleeing Cluaracan, cutting off any retreat to Knockmealldown.

The crowd of Folk, which had looked so large and bustling and mighty on the morning of the first day, now looked like a party of children in fancy dress as the Hëlhouses fell down all around them.

8.
NOLAN'S AXE

THE JUNGLE OF Hëlweed closed around me. I rolled back onto the road. Yellow shoots and red flowers were everywhere, squirming, moving and growing. They pushed against me and crowded around me. Occasionally a piece of house went flying past, a chunk of roof or a section of wall. All of Ghost Pig Estate must be one huge, heaving mass of Hëlweed now. I could hear the muffled roars and cries of the Folk as they were wrapped and trapped and tied and pinned. They would be swallowed and smothered and drowned soon.

I wondered if this had been the Cluaracan's plan all along. I didn't think so. I think he meant to go back to the Otherworld with Fester in his power and leave Knockmealldown empty of anything but birds to be devoured by the Hëlweed. He would have waited in silence for a thousand years until Fester gave in and told him she loved him. Or he would have gotten bored and fed her to the Hëlweed.

Tendrils wrapped themselves round my arms and legs and red flowers thrust themselves at my face. The stink that came from them was overwhelming. The stink of the Smell.

I couldn't imagine what it must be like for the Folk. They lived in high airy places, full of wind and the scents of flowers and leaves. Pollution was poison to them. Well, it was poison to us, too, but we were used to it.

I was used to the Smell. Three years. Three years since I took my first breath of it and it instantly coated the inside of my head and I had never been truly free of it since. Three years of it being in every mouthful of air, in every bite of food. Every word I spoke seemed to come out dripping with it. I wasn't completely immune to it but I had built up a resistance.

I tore my face away from the flower. I twisted and pulled and tugged against the yellow shoots. They tightened about me, but most of the energy of the Hëlweed was focused on subduing the Folk. I was just a weak human boy. I wasn't a threat to anyone.

I heaved and groaned and gritted my teeth. A tendril ripped. Yellow sap poured out. It stunk almost as badly as the flowers. I got an arm free, a leg. I wriggled and pulled and reached one hand across the hard red clay until my groping fingers found the handle of Taffe's Hammer.

Up above there were only a few scraps of sky left visible through the flowing and writhing weeds. I wrenched myself free, pulled the hurley upright and used it to stand. Breathing heavily, I took out the last piece of the Cloak and wound it around the shaft of the hurley. I held it firmly with both hands and turned it over so that the flat edge was facing out. It wasn't Mick Taffe's Hammer any more.

'You're Nolan's Axe now,' I told it.

I lifted it over my head and started to chop at the thick vines and branches. I swung left and right and straight ahead. Red flowers flew in pieces. Tendrils collapsed and spewed sap. They reached for me hungrily and I sliced them into pieces. I chopped my way towards the Folk, but the tendrils grew thicker until they were as big as tree trunks. I could crack them like eggs and splash sap everywhere but I could never batter through them, not without a chainsaw. I started to climb.

Up through thick layers of stalks wrapping themselves tighter and tighter. The poor Folk, trapped down there under all that! Thin branches grabbed at me, wrapped themselves around me and I chopped them down and flung them away. I was dripping with sap, covered in yellow bark, plastered with red petals. I couldn't feel the muscles in my arms any more.

Slipping, sliding, falling down into gaps between stalks, climbing out in a panic as they tried to crush me between them, lashing at the branches that came at me, weaker and weaker with every lash, no longer chopping, just knocking them away. Was I even going up any more? Was I just going round and round or deeper and deeper? I fell to my knees and leaned on the hurley. When I looked up again, I realised I had reached the top.

I took in great gasps of cleaner, clearer air. I drank in the clean blue sky and turned my face away from the glaring red eye of the setting sun. Knockmealldown rose on my left, utterly still and empty. The lake spread out on my right, the Floating Palace and the Island, and there was

something happening there, something I couldn't mak[...]
sense of. Loud angry machine noises on the boards and
the walks. Hooves battering on wood.

Never mind. No time for that. I was on the summit of a
writhing mass of invasive Otherworldly weed, and I could
feel it shifting below me as it opened a tunnel running
straight down, probing for my feet, ready to spring a trapdoor
and sending me screaming into the yellow darkness.

What could I do? What did I think I could do, one boy
and a hurley against a thing that had overwhelmed the
Folk?

But the hurley and me had friends. They were all flying
about on wings now, but if only they could remember,
if only they could hear me. Knockmealldowners to the
rescue.

I shakily stood up, the bark of the thick shoot below
cracking and breaking. I held up the hurley in both hands.

'HELP!' I screamed hoarsely. 'COME ON! YOU HAVE
TO HELP OR IT'S ALL OVER! YOU HAVE TO FIGHT!
TOGETHER! COME ON!'

The shoot below collapsed and I sank down up to my
knees. I could feel nothing under my feet and only the
tight squeeze of the knotted shoots kept me from plunging
down. But they were untying themselves, loosening. I
dropped down to my hips. Oh boy, I thought, too tired to
be scared. I let my arms fall and tried to anchor myself
with the hurley. I wasn't strong enough any more.

I heard a slow flap of wide wings, and two herons
landed gently in front of me and regarded my predicament
gravely.

'Hi guys,' I said, so incredibly happy to see them. 'Just in time.'

I crashed through the Hëlweed, down to my shoulders. 'Any chance of a wing out?' I asked.

A thousand wings rushed together and a hundred of every type of bird flew down out of the sky and settled on the Hëlweed and began to peck and pull and tear. They ripped and dragged and wrenched it apart, sending a great cloud of Hëlweed bits and pieces into the air around them. I felt the great mass of the thing shudder in shock.

A tiny wren fluttered and landed on the hurley. It hopped and pecked and studied it with a beady eye. Leaning sideways, it carefully examined the last piece of the Cloak. It gave a loud angry chirp and flew away again, into the churning horde of ripping beaks and claws.

Fester's friend, the Queen of the Birds who had given her the cloak. I don't know how I knew, but I knew.

Crack. My shoulders sank. My head was squeezed between my upraised arms, still holding grimly to the hurley. My feet kicked, looking for something to stand on, finding nothing. The herons spread their wings in consternation.

I felt the Hëlweed tremble and shake the way the ground trembles and shakes as a distant stampede gets closer. I thought it was just the Hëlweed fighting the birds but then the ghost pigs arrived, and Mulkytine. They galloped across the surface of the Hëlweed, the birds rising in a flapping flutter to let them pass, then settling back again to rip and tear. Darting and whirring around Mulkytine's head, leading him across the Hëlweed, was the tiny wren.

The herons flapped their wings and slowly lifted off, and Mulkytine turned in a skid that sent a fountain of sap and shoots and flowers flowing like a wave. The Hëlweed around me loosened and down I fell into the hollow space beneath, but a great tusked head thrust itself under the hurley and between my arms and heaved, and I was pulled out of the hole and tossed down the side of the disintegrating Hëlheap. I rolled and slid and thumped and bounced until I hit the road with a stunning jolt.

I lay there, spread-eagled, gasping, and had a perfect view of the Hëlheap slowly deflating as birds devoured it and the ghost pigs and Mulkytine trampled and tore it, until finally the distinct shapes of trapped Folk could be seen in the writhing mess, and they began to move and heave and struggle to free themselves. Somewhere along the way the Knockmealldowners were changed back. I felt almost ill with relief at the sight of human-shaped Bob and Shelia and Tom and Tricia and the others all pulling and fighting and kicking amongst the birds and pigs and Folk.

It was going to be a long, tedious process of stamping the last of the wriggling, twitching Hëlweed, and I had no time for it. I lurched to my feet and turned to the lake and ran as best I could to the Floating Palace. Not that I had any hope, not really. The Cluaracan would be long gone by now, and Fester and three quarters of the Cloak gone with him.

9.

PLAYING CHICKEN WITH HERONS

BUT THE CLUARACAN hadn't got far at all. He was on top of Fester in her pony form, forcing her to gallop up and down the walkways and over the bridges of the Floating Palace, pursued relentlessly and remorselessly by four figures on small, neat, fast motorbikes that buzzed along the ground like wasps, their long, shampooed and blow-dried hair streaming behind them, herding the Cluaracan and Fester back and forth, driving them away from the Isle. The Cluaracan's face was as red with rage as Fester's glowing eyes.

'You have more friends than you know, Brian Nolan,' said Lackley from beside me on the Green.

Two gasping, panting figures ran out of the storm of flattened Hëlweed. Their clothes and hair were plastered with sap and pieces of bark, and red petals clung to them all over. I probably looked the same.

'Hey, Brian!' said Helen. 'We've been pecking away at Hëlweed for the last ten minutes and it's so revolting I don't think I could eat another vegetable again ever as long as I live!'

'I was a bird,' said Derek in a voice of solemn childish amazement. 'Brian, I had wings and feathers and a beak and everything and I was flying, Brian. In the sky, Brian. I was flying in the sky.'

He seemed completely dazed. Helen looked at him pityingly.

'Come on,' she said. 'This'll make you feel better.'

'What are you talkin' about? It felt—'

Helen grabbed him by one arm and me by the other and dragged us into the water of the lake. We fell and splashed and the shock of the cold woke us and refreshed us and took most of the Hëlweed off of us, and cleared our heads and our noses of the Smell. I could have stayed in there forever, but even ten seconds was too long. I dragged them back out again and pointed at the Palace and the cat-and-mouse between the Cluaracan, Fester and the banshees.

'Them bikes don't hold much gas,' said Derek. 'They won't be able to keep that up for long.'

'Let's get him then,' said Helen, and we ran for the Floating Palace. There were people and Folk running down from the Estate behind us, everybody rushing and yelling in a confusion of excitement and exhilaration. Two herons lifted off and flew towards me.

Was that Mum and Dad? Why weren't they changed back with everyone else?

No. I must have imagined it.

The bikes were still buzzing and hooves were clattering furiously on the Floating Palace. The Cluaracan was nearly there. As we watched, Fester shattered one of the bikes with a deadly flying hoof. A wheel spun in the air and bounced on the walkway. The banshee sat splay-legged beside the wreck, shaking her head, making her silky hair tumble and toss.

'Why are they helping us?' I asked.

'Because you were nice to them, barnacle-brain,' said Helen. 'Nobody's ever nice to *them*.'

Three bikes zipped back and forth between the Cluaracan and the far end of the Floating Palace, charging, dodging, herding, blocking. We went over a high bridge and saw them across a stretch of water. The banshees had them cornered, with two blocking the boardwalk ahead and another parked across the way behind. The Cluaracan kicked his heels into Fester's flanks and she gave a terrible scream of rage. She ducked her head and shook her mane, her red eyes blazing. There was no sign of our strange feathery friend, and no sign that she recognised us. The Cluaracan was in complete control now. She charged, hooves shattering boards like falling rocks. The two bikes and banshees were knocked aside as if they were toys, crashing through the railing into the lake. Fester galloped away, the third banshee revving her engine in pursuit.

I sprinted like mad, forgetting everyone and everything. My lungs were as flat and crumpled as empty crisp packets and the stitch in my side was put there by a needle the size of the Spire in Dublin City. I had to get to the Isle before the Cluaracan. There was no way I could get to the Isle before the Cluaracan.

Swooping out of the sky came a pair of long-legged, long-beaked herons. They cut like arrows, flying straight and level and true, right at the Cluaracan.

He stared them down. He urged Fester on. He didn't flinch or move or duck, and they didn't change course by a centimetre. He must have been able to see their eyes, peering calm and determined, and they must have seen all the veins on his round red nose when he suddenly threw his arms up in front of his face and with a high-pitched scream flung himself sideways, off Fester's back, over the railing and into the water.

The herons shot over Fester's head, nearly clipping an ear each. The Cluaracan, sitting dry on the water as if it was a lawn or a carpet, looked back at us, humans and Folk all scattered across the lake and the Palace. The King and Queen were charging along the shore surrounded by a furious blaze of green light. Fester was galloping around a long curve and a turn that was bringing her to me. The Cluaracan shook his head as if mildly disappointed at the way things had fallen out, and started jogging across the waves to the Isle.

'Aw, that's not fair,' said Derek, sounding utterly exhausted. 'Who told him he could walk on water?'

'That shouldn't be allowed at all,' said Helen.

Fester slid to a halt when she saw me, all four hooves sliding on the boards; I ran up to her with my arms out but she screeched in that horrible way only horses can screech, and reared, nearly taking my head off with her hooves. Helen and Derek were on either side of me, and we stretched out our arms and called her name until she calmed down. Helen patted her head and stroked her neck and whispered in her ear. She nodded at Derek, who pushed me forward and bent down and linked his hands together.

'Up you get,' he said. 'Run that slurryhead down.'

I put one foot on his linked hands and he heaved me onto Fester's back. She turned and stamped and I grabbed her mane.

'If it's okay with you,' I said. 'Let's go run that slurryhead down.'

She neighed, and it sounded like a laugh.

10.

THE CLOAK OF FEATHERS

FESTER AND I ran down the walkways and over the bridges and through the platforms, the last banshee on her bike sputtering behind us, the herons circling low overhead. We climbed the steps that went up and around Long Lisa's Tower, crows scattering wildly in all directions, and we caught him in the pavilion, about to head down the steps to the beach where I'd woken that morning.

From the beach he could have slipped through the hawthorns to the gateway that led back to the Otherworld. Instead, he was backing slowly away from the steps as we clattered in, and he had his hands held out in front of him. Because up the stairs came Mulkytine, snuffling and snorting and twitching his head this way and that so his tusks jabbed at the Cluaracan, forcing him back.

I slid down off Fester and stalked up to the Cluaracan, breathing so hard I could barely speak, so full of anger I could barely think. I didn't even remember to be scared of him.

'Can't a fella have a minute's peace round here without being mobbed by well-wishers?' said the Cluaracan in a y voice. 'Well, you have me. Here I am. What is it you want of me?'

'I WIN!' I roared, incandescent, poking him in the chest with the hurley. 'I won! We beat your lousy rotten Hëlhouses. We caught you. We won. The Challenge is over. I want that Cloak. I won it fair and square! I can see it in your coat. Give it to me! NOW!'

The banshee revved the bike behind me and Mulkytine squealed and Fester whinnied. None of it seemed to faze the Cluaracan. He gave a charming little laugh.

'My coat, is it? Well, it's a fine coat indeed and I've had it for an age, so I'll be cold without it. But a Challenge is a Challenge and no gentleman reneges on a Challenge. That's what honour is, young Brian. Here it is. Wear it well, and may it give you joy.'

He slipped it off and I snatched it out of his hands and turned to Fester, who was standing, trembling, beside me. I draped it over her back and slipped the first piece of the Cloak, the one we'd found in the library, off the hurley and put it over the coat. I hoped I wouldn't have to sew them together or anything because I couldn't feel my fingers any more.

'There,' I said. 'Now. There it is.'

Nothing happened.

'I don't think it's cut for her style at all,' drawled the Cluaracan. I pulled the coat back off, and groped inside. The lining was smooth – silk or linen or something like that. Not feathers. No feathers at all. I looked at the Cluaracan. Over his shirt he was wearing a waistcoat, the same style and cut as the coat.

'That waistcoat,' I said. 'It's in the waistcoat.'

'Ah, you asked for the coat, not for the waistcoat. Ne
you'll be wanting to have the shirt off me back! If you want
the waistcoat, get your own. I'm all tapped out and I've
learned me lessons about the evils o' gamblin'.'

'No,' I said. 'I must have the Cloak! I won't give up, I
won't, I won't . . .'

'Lad,' said the Cluaracan softly. 'You won. Fair play.
You'll get your parents back, curse their beaks, and you
saved the village, may all their doors jam. Don't push it.
Let it go.'

The banshee had dismounted and was floating across
the pavilion towards him, and Mulkytine was pawing the
boards and lowering his head, ready to charge. Derek and
Helen came running in, and behind them the King and
Queen and a gaggle of Folk and 'Downers. They were
a raging mob ready to rip him apart. Fester reared up
and drove them back. Derek and Helen dodged round
her but everyone else fell back. The Cluaracan was still
driving her.

Derek and Helen and me closed around him. He
unbuttoned the waistcoat with one hand, and held it open.
He lifted his other hand and it was running with blue
flames.

'A step nearer and I burn it,' he said. 'It'll be ashes and
she'll never be free, she'll never find her own shape and
she'll lose her mind to the will of the *púca*!'

'No,' I said, desperately. I dropped the hurley and
started to babble, not sure what I was saying. 'No, no, no!
Don't! Cluaracan! Listen! Do you know what she told me?

told me she wanted to go back to you. She told me she
anted to tell you she was sorry, that she was wrong, that
she should have said yes when you asked for her hand a
hundred years ago. She said she wished she hadn't hurt
you the way she did, that she had been too ashamed to say
anything sooner, and that now she doesn't dare because
she thinks you won't believe her and that she's trying to
trick you. She loves you, Cluaracan. She'll marry you.'

A heavy silence had fallen in the pavilion as everyone
waited.

'She loves me not,' said the Cluaracan. 'You lie, or she
lies. Let her tell me herself so I can throw her lies back at
her.'

'She can't tell you – you've made a horse of her!' said
Derek.

'It's true – she wouldn't speak of anything else!' said
Helen. 'All she'd talk about was how much she regretted
saying no to you!'

The Cluaracan glared at us, his face twisted and ugly,
then he looked at Fester, and hesitated. He reached out for
her with his burning hand. The flames vanished and he
took a step towards her.

'Now,' said Helen, and we leaped on him. I grabbed
the neck of the waistcoat and pulled with all my might,
while Helen and Derek grabbed his arms. I heard a rip
and buttons popped and flew. The waistcoat came away in
my hands, but the Cluaracan was pulled backwards and
fell, and I fell under him. All the breath was knocked out
of me and I was pinned to the boards by his weight and
the weight of Helen and Derek. The waistcoat was caught

between me and the Cluaracan and I pulled and yanke
it to get it free while the three of them fought and punch
and kicked and twisted on top of me.

'I'll turn you all into maggots, you maggots!' he roared.
The blue flames erupted from his hand again and he
reached for my face. 'Get off me!'

Helen and Derek grabbed hold of his arm with one
hand each and held the burning hand back from my
face. I could feel the flicker of hot flame prickle my skin.
I tried to scrabble away and out from under them. I
heaved at the waistcoat. Helen and Derek strained to keep
the burning hand away but I could feel my skin start to
roast.

'You're mine!' I croaked at the Cloak. 'I won you, you're
mine! By right of the Challenge and the Four Feats! I claim
you!'

With a terrific tearing rip the waistcoat came apart in
my hands. Suddenly feathers were whirling and flying all
around us.

'No!' The Cluaracan's flaming hand flickered out.
He shook Helen and Derek off and jumped to his feet,
grabbing at the feathers blowing around us like a dark
snowstorm. 'No! Come back! You're mine!'

'No!' I said, pushing myself upright with great effort. 'I
won it from you and it's mine! And I'm giving it to her!'

I pointed at Fester.

The storm of feathers rushed around and around, faster and
faster, in a whirlwind that closed around us, hundreds
and hundreds of feathers spinning wildly, shimmering and
shining. They suddenly swept down on Fester, gathering

melting together, like smoke, drifting over her shoulders and flowing down her back.

The feathers swirled and settled, merging with the other parts of the Cloak on Fester's back, becoming a thick layer that fluttered and shook, and Fester changed. Faster than the blinking of an eye, Fester the strange dark horse with the glowing red eyes was gone, and in her place was a tall, unearthly girl with skin the green of a sunlit field and small curling horns and teeth that seemed sharp and eyes that were as dark as midnight pools. She lifted her arms over her head and jumped into the air.

The Queen cried out and the King swore, and they wept and laughed and wept some more and held each other and watched as their long-lost daughter returned to them. The Folk roared.

'YES!' yelled Fester. 'I'm me, I'm me, I'm me again! You wormy old Cluaracan you! May you run and never stop running! All things will hunt you across all worlds and you will never know rest until the end of all things!'

The Cluaracan blanched, as grey as cold porridge.

'You Highness,' he said. 'I never meant . . . I only wanted . . . it was just a . . .'

'Oh, don't go wittering and wilting now, you big greasy lump. Mulkytine, my old friend! Perhaps you and your family there should be the first to sport with him! Here's the one who built the factory that poisoned the air and the water and made meals of you all! Here's the one who built the lonely empty houses with no souls and no hearts! Leave off your haunting of this place and run free where you like!'

The Cluaracan must have got the gist of where this was going, because he was already pounding down the stairs towards the little beach. Mulkytine squealed and clattered after him, and across the waters came a line of charging ghost pigs. The Cluaracan plunged into the thick hawthorn jungle until he reached the clearing at the middle with the circle of standing stones and leaped into the centre of the circle and vanished. Mulkytine and the ghost pigs all followed, hot on his heels, disappearing into the Otherworld.

'That'll keep him busy for a while,' said Fester, wiping her hands. 'And I hope I never see the miserable moon-faced slapgullion again.'

She turned to Helen and Derek and me, but before any of us could say anything the King and the Queen had her, and wrapping her in their arms with cries of wonder and delight and disbelief.

Then my own parents came running into the pavilion, human again, and did pretty much the same thing with me. Bob clapped Derek on the back and Sheila gathered him in a hug. Helen rolled her eyes a little, but grinned as Sheila reached out to include her. All over the lake and the Palace the Folk were going wild as the news spread, and the Knockmealldowners were pretty happy about things, too.

The Princess left her parents and walked over to me and extracted me from mine. She smiled at me.

'Hey, Brian,' she said.

'Hey, uh, Princess,' I said.

'Call me Fester.'

'You sure?'

'Only to my friends.'

'Okay, then. Fester.'

'So, what we usually do here is grant the guy who saved the Princess a wish. Do you want to make a wish Brian?'

'Um,' I said. 'There is one thing.'

'Name it.'

'Well . . .'

'Yes?'

'You don't all have to go back now, do you?'

Her eyes twinkled, full of stars.

'No,' she said. 'We don't.'

'Do you think we could we have a proper Great Festival? For one day?'

'Brian,' she said. 'That's the best wish I ever heard anyone ask for.'

I grinned.

'Great,' said Helen. 'But just so you know, I'm resigning from the Committee.'

'D'you think I could be a bird again?' Derek asked, wistfully. 'Just for a while?'

Part Four: Another Day

1.

THE GREAT FESTIVAL

THE NEXT DAY, we had a Festival.

It was Great.

I mean, really Great.

We had music. We had dancing. We had sport and we had craic. We laughed so hard our sides were sore. We sang so loud our vocal chords went on strike. We had food so lovely we almost passed out at each mouthful.

We had family, neighbours, and guests, and most important of all we had friends, and we were all together.

It was amazing. The best Festival in the country. The world. The entire flippin' universe.

2.

THE DAY BEFORE ONE HUNDRED YEARS

THE NEXT DAY, we all stood together by the lake of Lisashee. They didn't want to go. We didn't want them to go.

The Folk gathered in a large host, all who were returning. Some were heading out into the world to see what it had to offer. The Knockmealldowners stood and watched. The dense tangle of hawthorn had drawn back to allow us all to crowd around the stone circle. A silence fell across the Isle of Lisashee.

The Queen made a graceful gesture of welcome with an outstretched hand. The little dog came forward, dragging the auld fella at the end of the length of blue string. The auld fella's head was bowed and his feet dragged and his bow hung from one hand. His fiddle was now somewhere at the bottom of the lake, and enchanted with it. The Queen presented him with a new one, shiny and clean. The auld fella blinked and smiled and held it close to his chest.

'Thank you! Thank you!' barked the dog, dancing and jumping with joy.

'No, thank you,' said the King, drying his eyes. 'We'll be off now. Thanks for a great Great Festival. Sorry about all the, well – you know. Enjoy the next hundred years, and we'll be seeing you then!'

The Queen made no speech, but she stopped next to me and touched me gently on the cheek.

'Thank you for saving our daughter,' she said. 'Thank you for saving us. Thank you for saving the Festival. To you our doors will always be open.'

Led by the King and Queen, the Other Folk, all waving goodbyes, giving last hugs and embraces, vanished into the circle of stones.

The Princess was last to go. She gave each of us a long hug. She didn't say a word, but before she went, she looked at me, and winked.

Mulligans and Traceys, visitors and natives, left-behind Folk in careful disguises, all walked together across the Floating Palace back to the village. The sun shone down on Knockmealldown, gentle and benign. Mum and Dad and Bob and Sheila would be having a well-deserved rest and a break, and would get treated like royalty for the rest of their lives.

With a rumble of thunder and a cloud of exhaust, the four banshees rode out of Knockmealldown and into the roads of the wide world.

The Great Festival was over. But the magic would never really go away, living on in our memories and our hearts.

And it would all come back in another hundred years.

The Floating Palace would stay, and visitors would be permitted, so long as the Isle was left untouched. It was the domain of Lackley and Mullcytine, and they would guard it and protect it.

Ghost Pig Estate – all the empty haunted houses, the toxic Smell and the Hëlweed – was gone. Only our house was left, standing all alone in a torn-up field. Mum and Dad were already planning on turning it into a community farm. One or two of the Hëlhouses had escaped, though, and had last been seen fleeing into the hills.

Everyone knows next year's Festival won't be Great, but it'll still be pretty good.

Derek and Helen and me stayed behind at Lisashee after everyone else was gone. We stood on the tiny beach and watched Knockmealldown settle back into peace and quiet across the glimmering water.

'You must be exhausted,' said Helen.

'All that running around doin' Challenges and Feats, fighting Hëlweed and whatever,' said Derek. 'It'd wear anyone out.'

'You need a rest after all that,' said Helen. 'Slow down and take it easy.'

'Yeah,' I said. They were right. But in my mind I saw the circle of stones in the shadow of the Tower of Long Lisa Lenane. Their doors would never be closed to me.

'I was just thinking, though. I'd like to see how Fester is doing. I'd like to make sure they're still keeping the Cluaracan on the run. I'd like to see the Otherworld. Wouldn't you?'

I turned and grinned at them.

'Well . . .' said Helen thoughtfully. 'Now that the Festival is over I don't really have anything else to do . . . why not?'

'Oh yeah,' said Derek. 'It's only been five minutes and I'm bored brainless already.'